PRESS START

D0963015

jF
Terrell,
Brandon

WRITTEN BY
BRANDON TERRELL

COVER AND INTERIOR ILLUSTRATED BY
EDUARDO FERRARA

COVER COLORS BY
OVERDRIVE STUDIO AT
SPACE GOAT PRODUCTIONS

INTERIOR COLORS BY
KOMIKAKI STUDIO
FEATURING SAW33 AT
SPACE GOAT PRODUCTIONS

LETTERING BY
JAYMES REED

SI KIDS Graphic Novels are published by Stone Arch Books,
a Capstone Imprint
1710 Roe Crest Drive
North Mankato, Minnesota 56003
www.capstonepub.com

Text © 2015
Illustrations © 2015 Stone Arch Books

Library of Congress Cataloging-in-Publication Data is
available on the Library of Congress website.

ISBN: 978-1-4342-4164-1 (library binding)
ISBN: 978-1-4342-9181-3 (paperback

Ashley C. Andersen Zantop PUBLISHER
Michael Dahl EDITORIAL DIRECTOR
Sean Tulien EDITOR
Heather Kindseth CREATIVE DIRECTOR
Brann Garvey ART DIRECTOR
Hilary Wacholz DESIGNER

Summary: Jared Richards is undefeated in baseball
games—video games, anyway. But when he loses a bet to
his best friend, Jared is forced to get off the couch and step
onto the field for his school's baseball team tryouts. Jared
ends up being pretty impressive as a pitcher—until the line
between video games and reality begins to blur. Can Jared
sort out the glitch in his brain before he blows the big game?

Printed in the United States of America in Stevens Point, Wisconsin.
032014   008092WZF14

Sports Illustrated KIDS

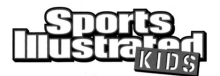

PRESENTS

8-BIT BASEBALL

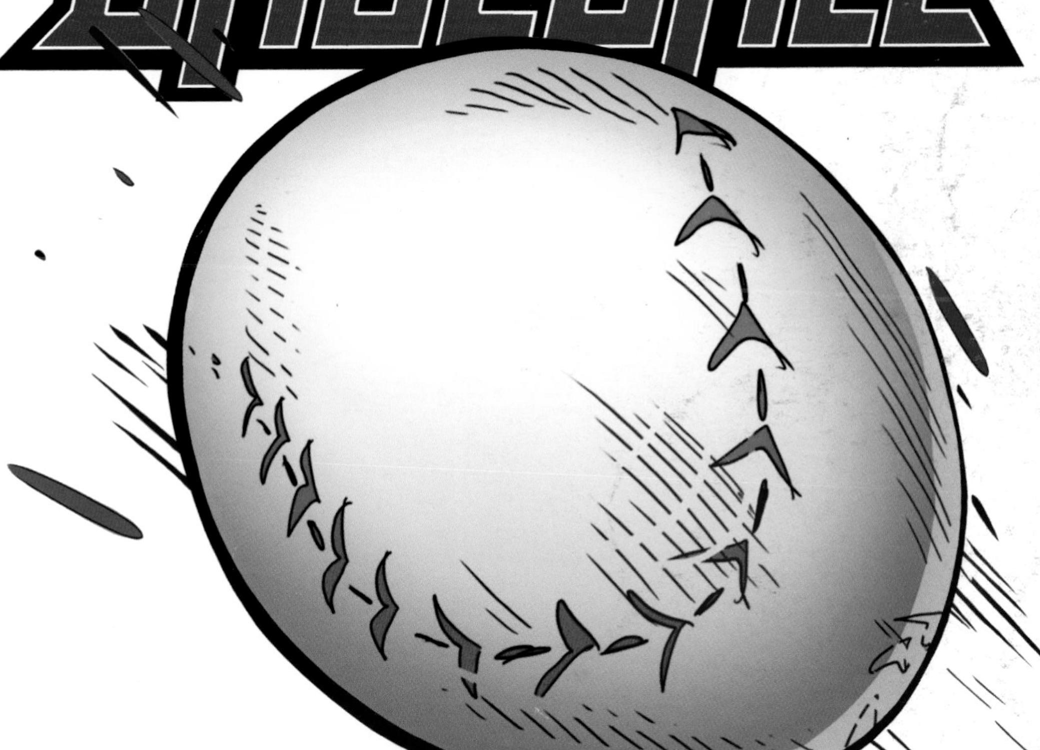

STONE ARCH BOOKS
A Capstone Imprint

SELECT PLAYER

Jared Richards

HEIGHT: 4 feet, 11 inches

FEARS: losing

FAVORITE BOOKS: Jake Maddox sports novels

WEIGHT: 108 pounds

TEAM: Tornadoes

SKILLS: video games, ignoring homework, and being late to class

Cole Daniels

HEIGHT: 5 feet, 6 inches

FEARS: spiders

FAVORITE BOOK: Cole doesn't read

WEIGHT: 155 pounds

TEAM: Crows

SKILLS: swinging bats, tallying home runs and taking names

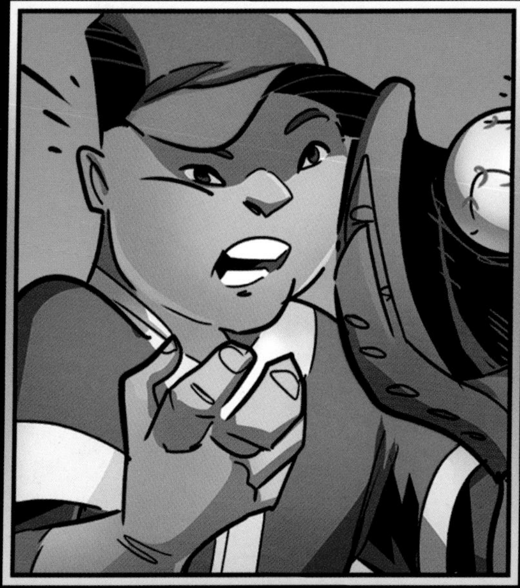

Joe Akido

HEIGHT: 4 feet, 8 inches

FEARS: spicy food and cats

FAVORITE BOOK: Mr. Puzzle

WEIGHT: 90 pounds

TEAM: Tornadoes

SKILLS: speed, strength, and getting dirty on the field

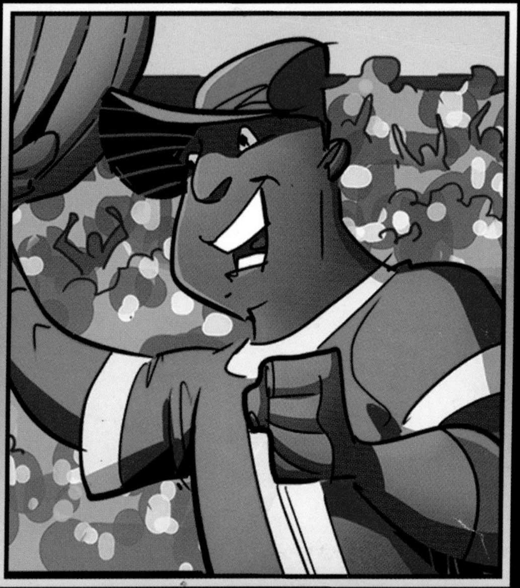

Malcolm Harding

HEIGHT: 5 feet, 4 inches

FEARS: scary movies

FAVORITE BOOKS: DC Super Heroes Comic Chapter Books

WEIGHT: 112 pounds

TEAM: Tornadoes

SKILLS: has encyclopedic knowledge of everything comic-book related

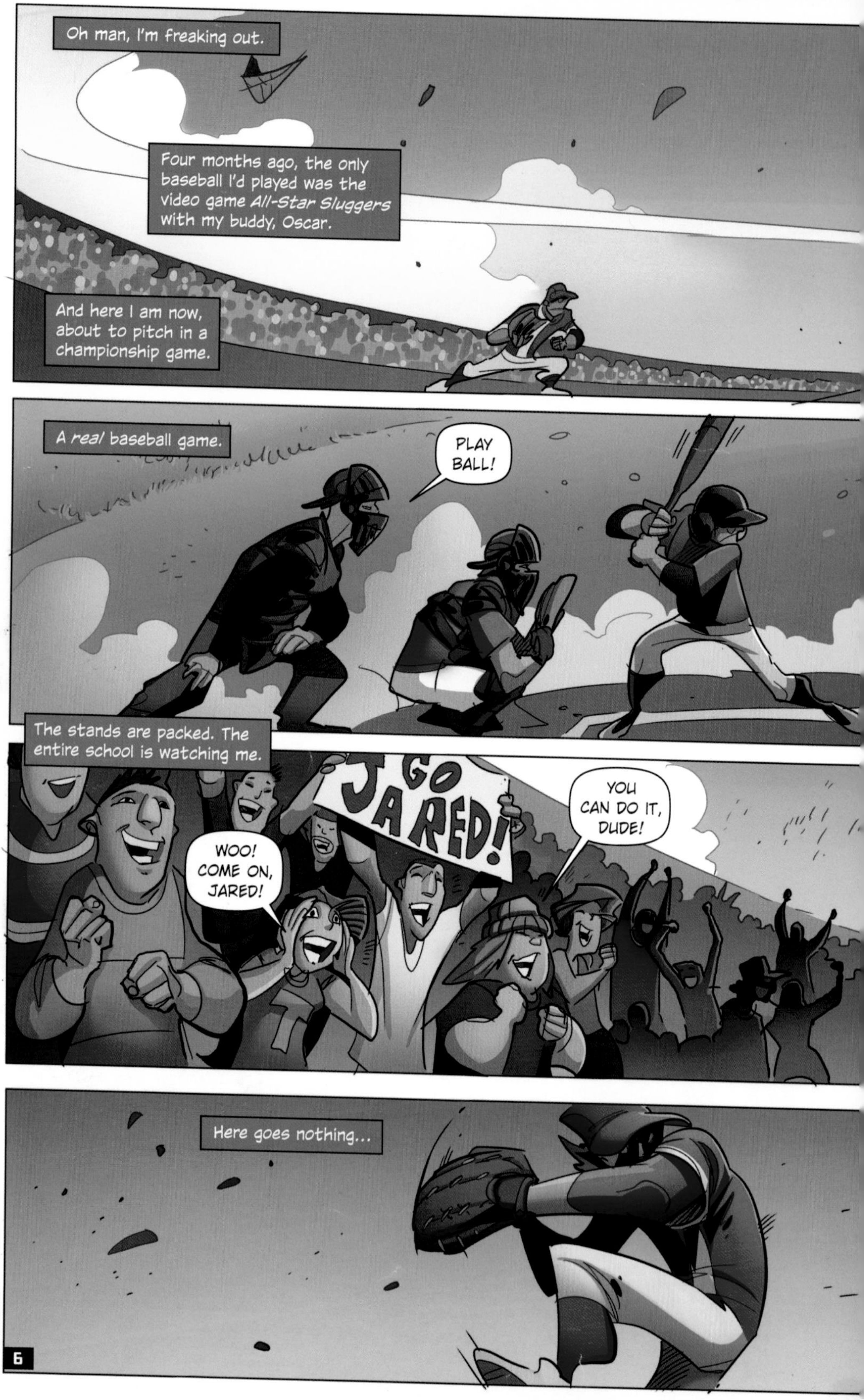
Oh man, I'm freaking out.
Four months ago, the only baseball I'd played was the video game *All-Star Sluggers* with my buddy, Oscar.
And here I am now, about to pitch in a championship game.
A *real* baseball game.
PLAY BALL!
The stands are packed. The entire school is watching me.
GO JARED!
WOO! COME ON, JARED!
YOU CAN DO IT, DUDE!
Here goes nothing...

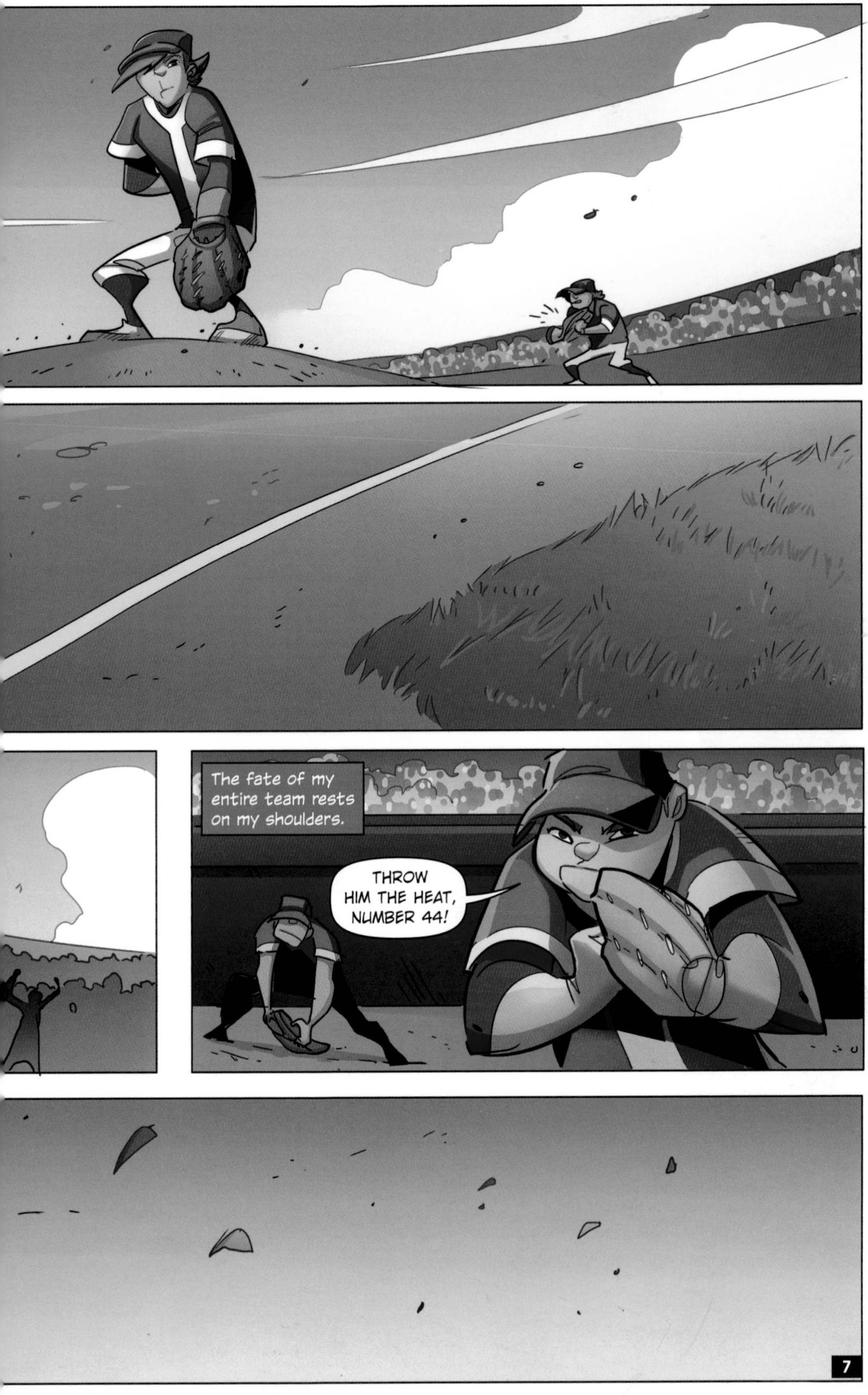
The fate of my entire team rests on my shoulders.
THROW HIM THE HEAT, NUMBER 44!

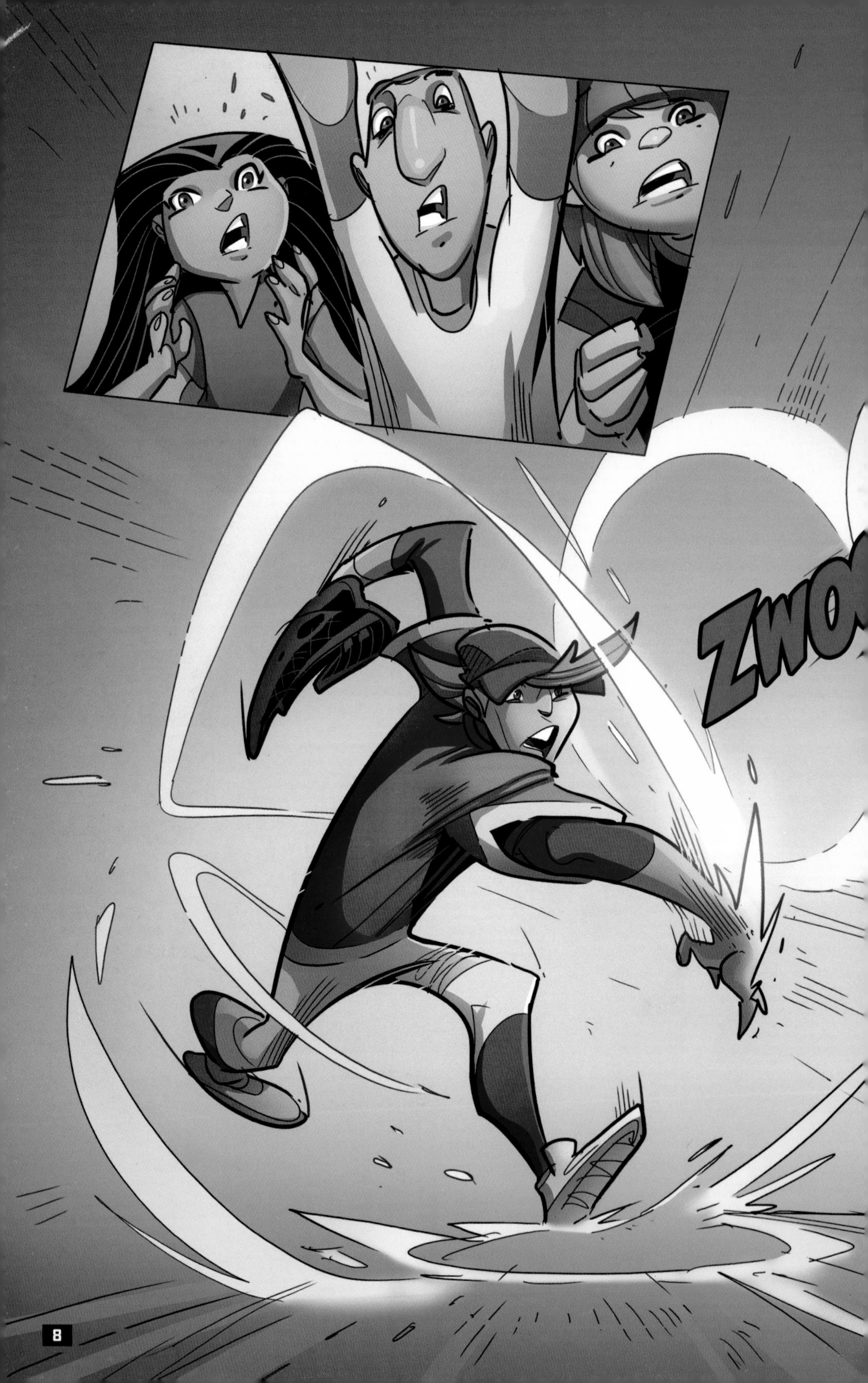
ZWO

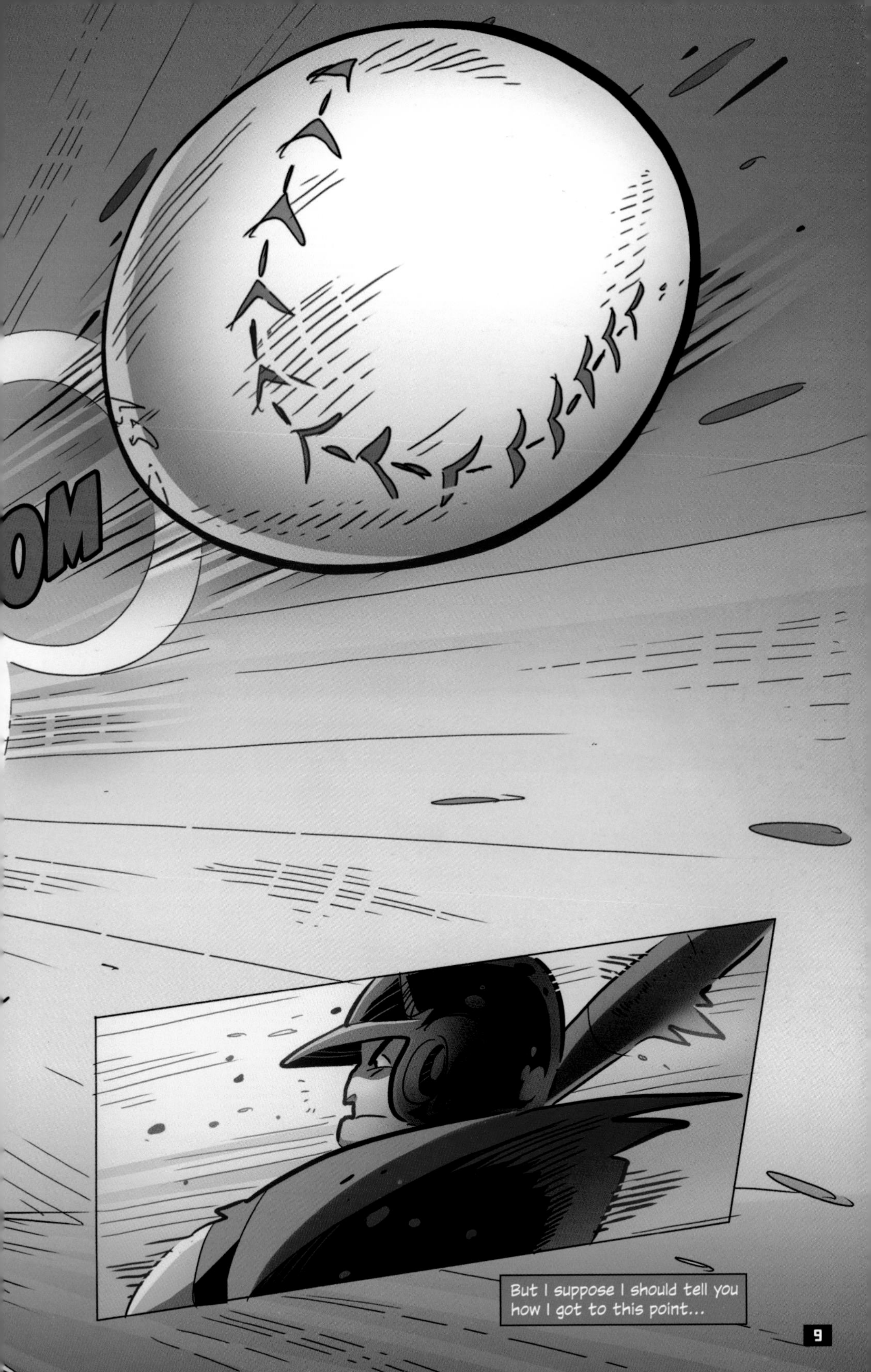
But I suppose I should tell you how I got to this point...

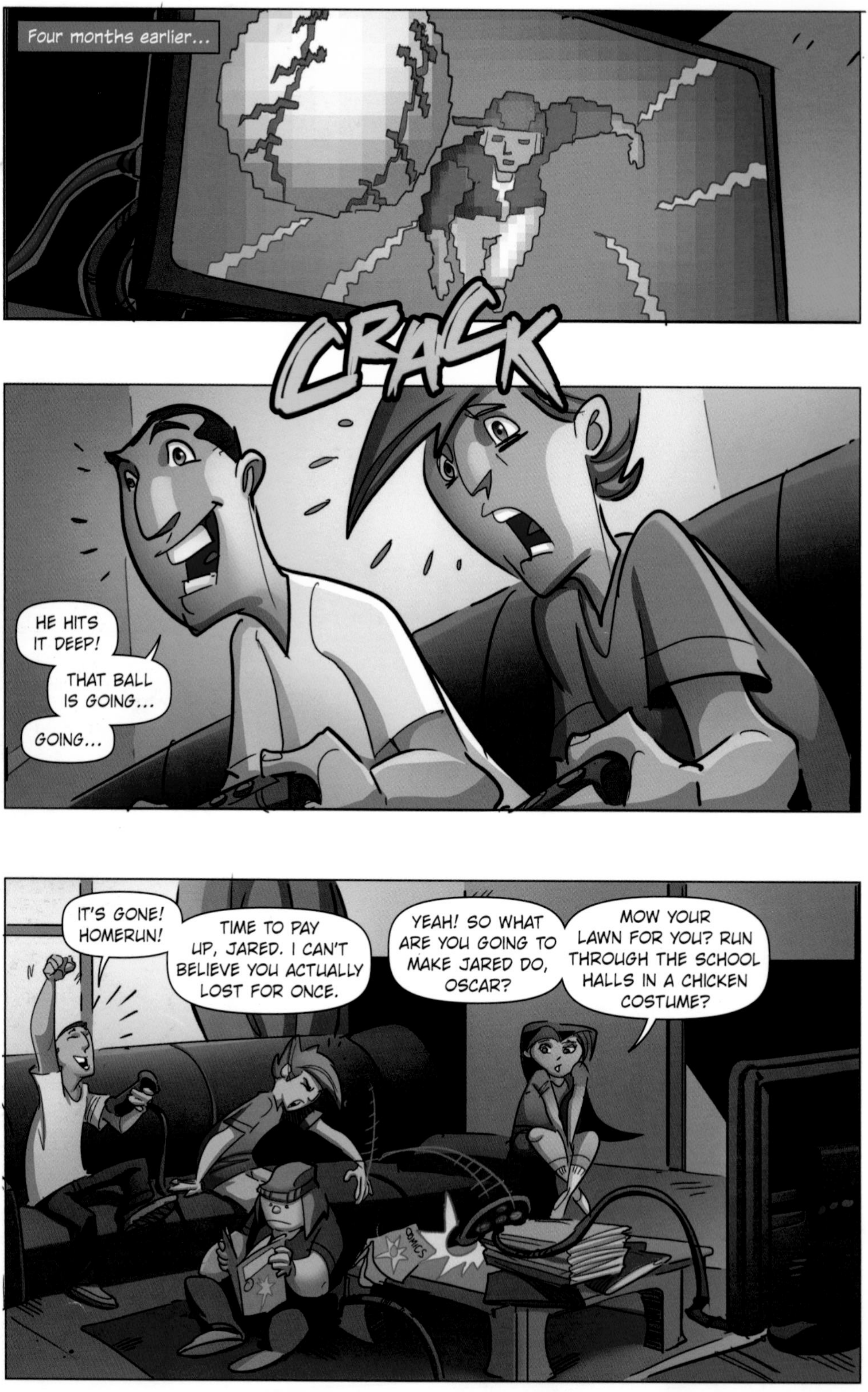
Four months earlier...
CRACK
HE HITS IT DEEP!
THAT BALL IS GOING...
GOING...
IT'S GONE! HOMERUN!
TIME TO PAY UP, JARED. I CAN'T BELIEVE YOU ACTUALLY LOST FOR ONCE.
YEAH! SO WHAT ARE YOU GOING TO MAKE JARED DO, OSCAR?
MOW YOUR LAWN FOR YOU? RUN THROUGH THE SCHOOL HALLS IN A CHICKEN COSTUME?
COMICS

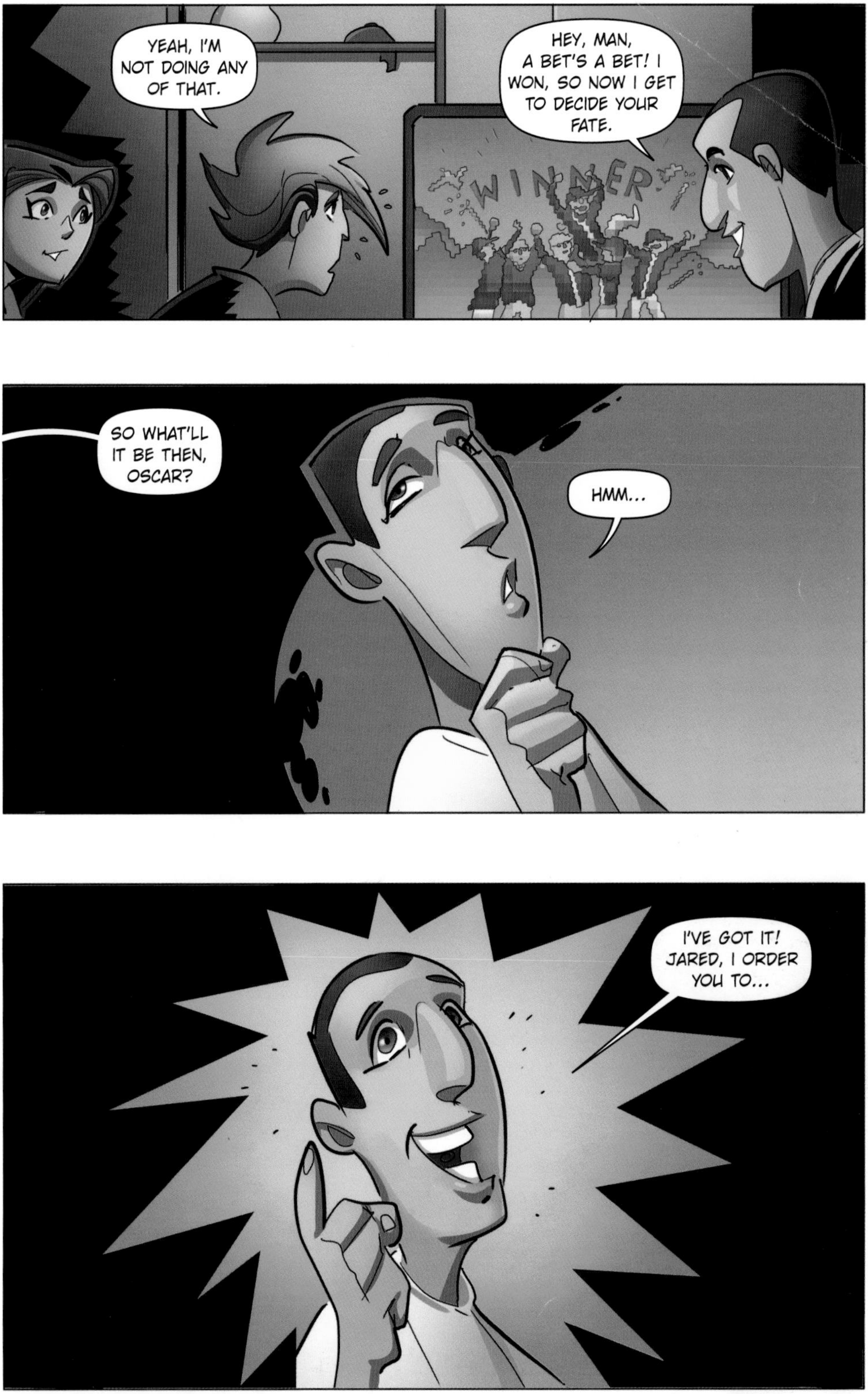
YEAH, I'M NOT DOING ANY OF THAT.
HEY, MAN, A BET'S A BET! I WON, SO NOW I GET TO DECIDE YOUR FATE.
WINNER
SO WHAT'LL IT BE THEN, OSCAR?
HMM...
I'VE GOT IT! JARED, I ORDER YOU TO...

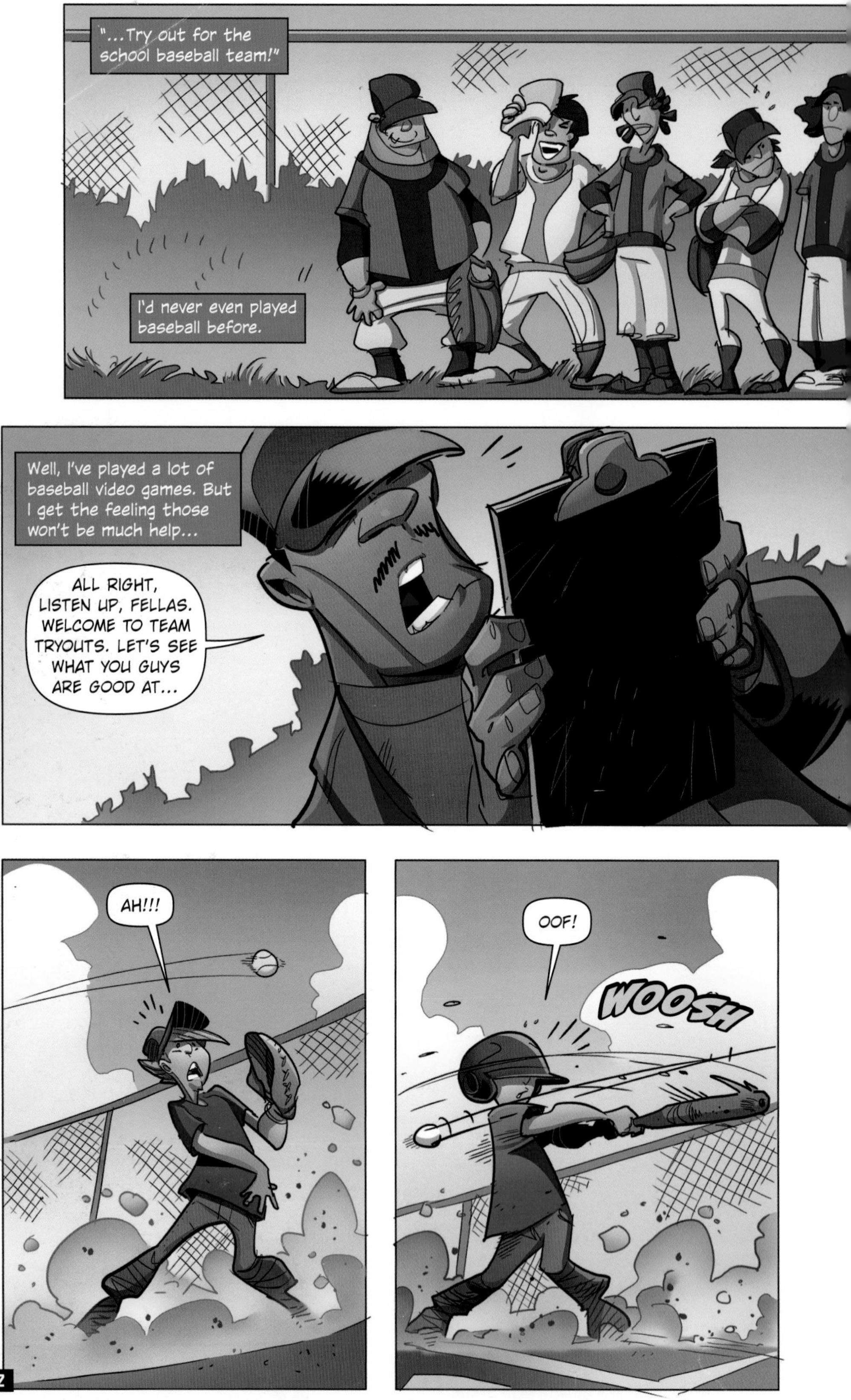
"...Try out for the school baseball team!"
I'd never even played baseball before.
Well, I've played a lot of baseball video games. But I get the feeling those won't be much help...
ALL RIGHT, LISTEN UP, FELLAS. WELCOME TO TEAM TRYOUTS. LET'S SEE WHAT YOU GUYS ARE GOOD AT...
AH!!!
OOF!
WOOSH

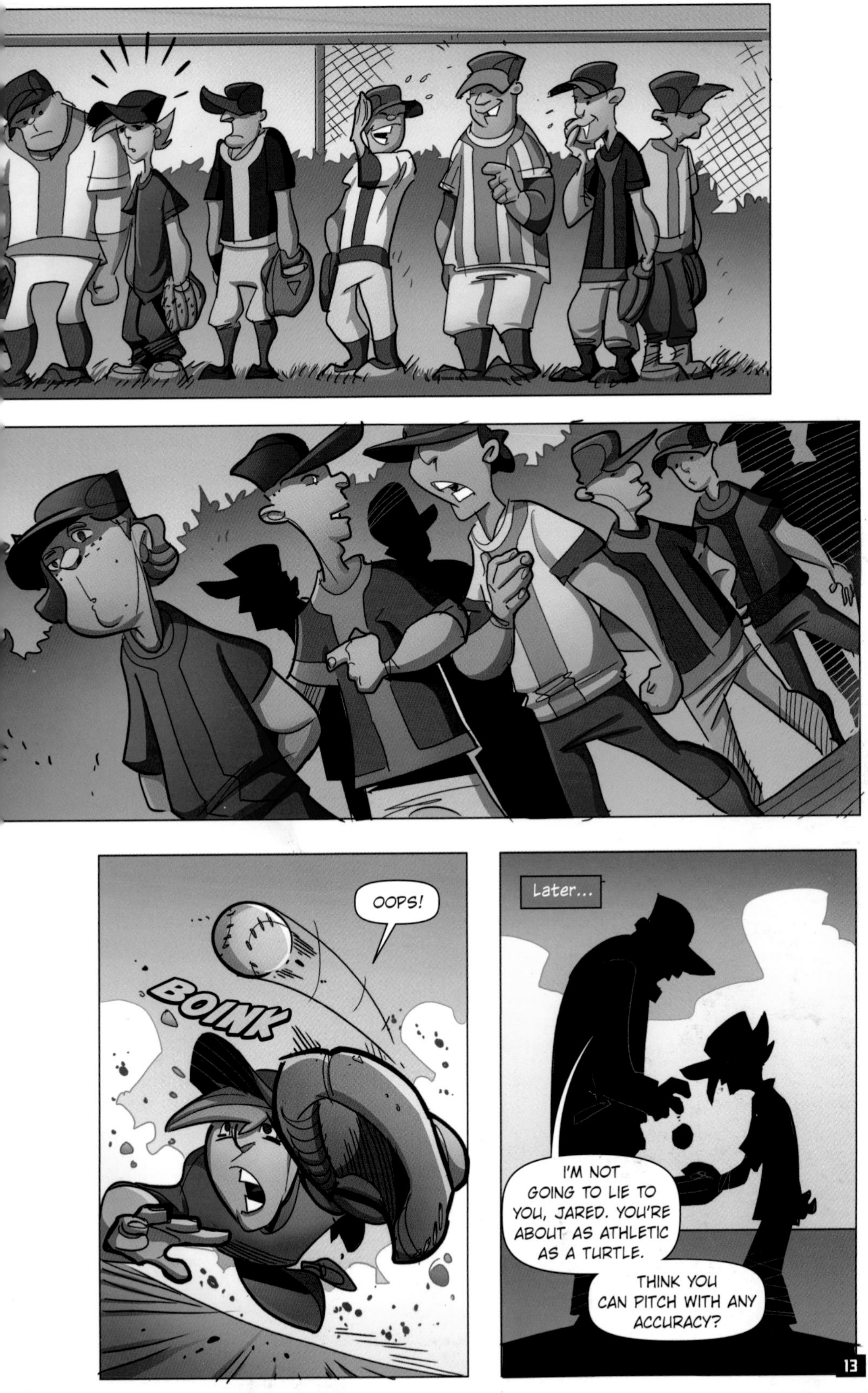

OOPS!
BOINK
Later...
I'M NOT GOING TO LIE TO YOU, JARED. YOU'RE ABOUT AS ATHLETIC AS A TURTLE.
THINK YOU CAN PITCH WITH ANY ACCURACY?

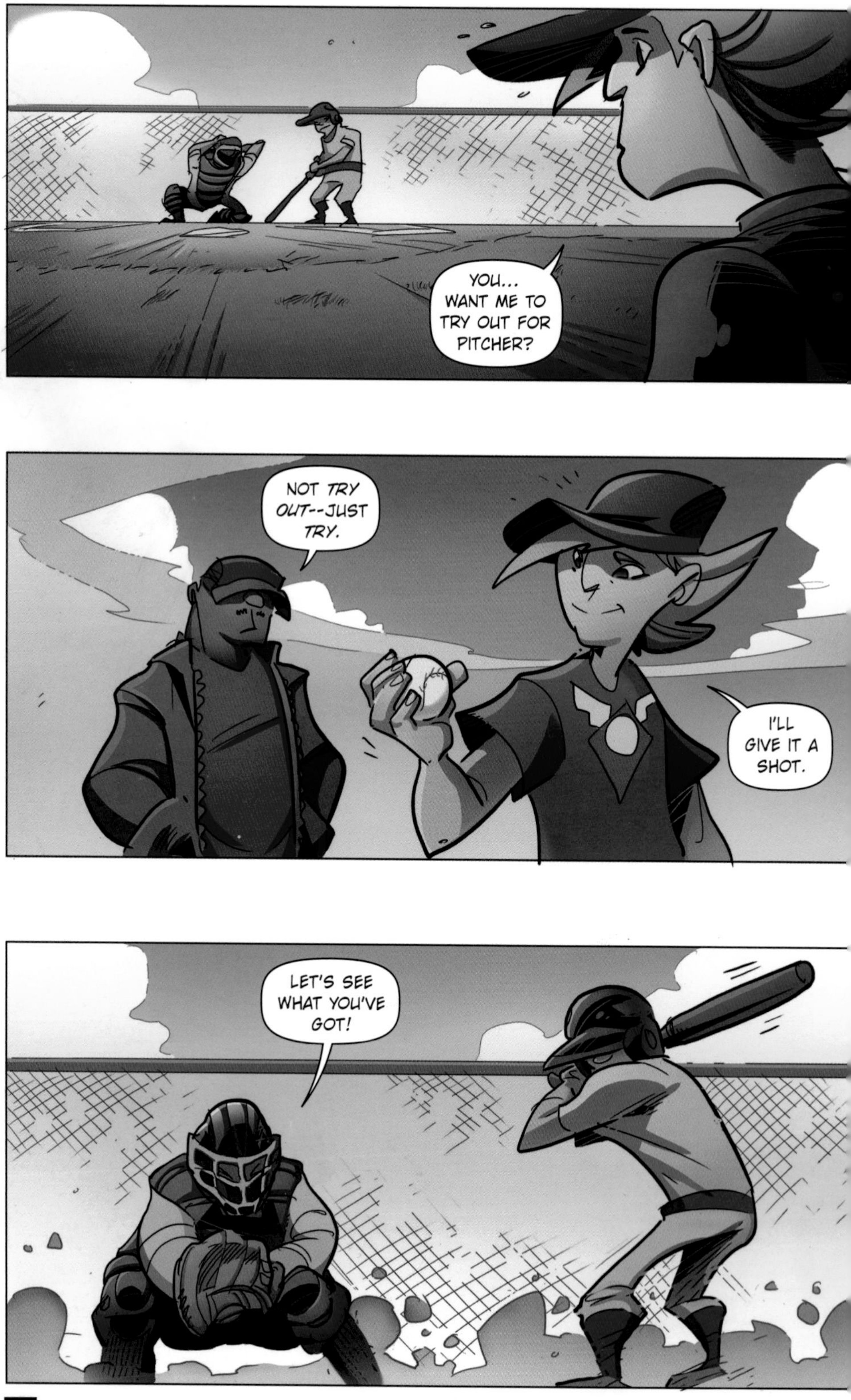
YOU... WANT ME TO TRY OUT FOR PITCHER?
NOT TRY OUT--JUST TRY.
I'LL GIVE IT A SHOT.
LET'S SEE WHAT YOU'VE GOT!

ZWOOOOM
WOW!
THUMP
HUH. NOT BAD.
THANKS.
I found out later this was coach Fenton's excited face.
And that's how I made the team.

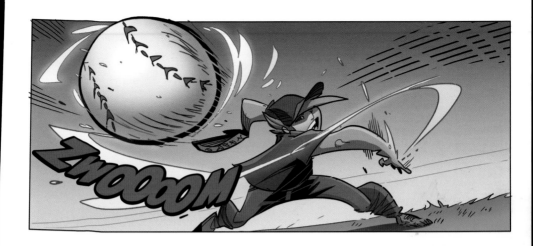

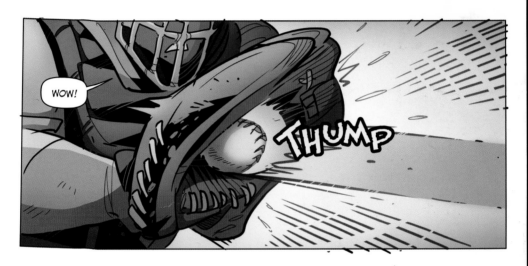

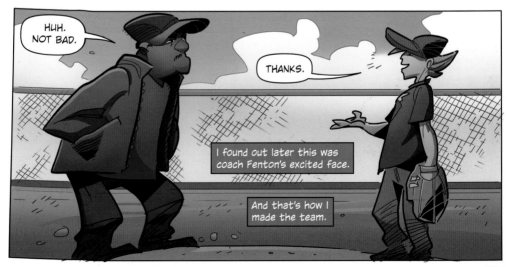

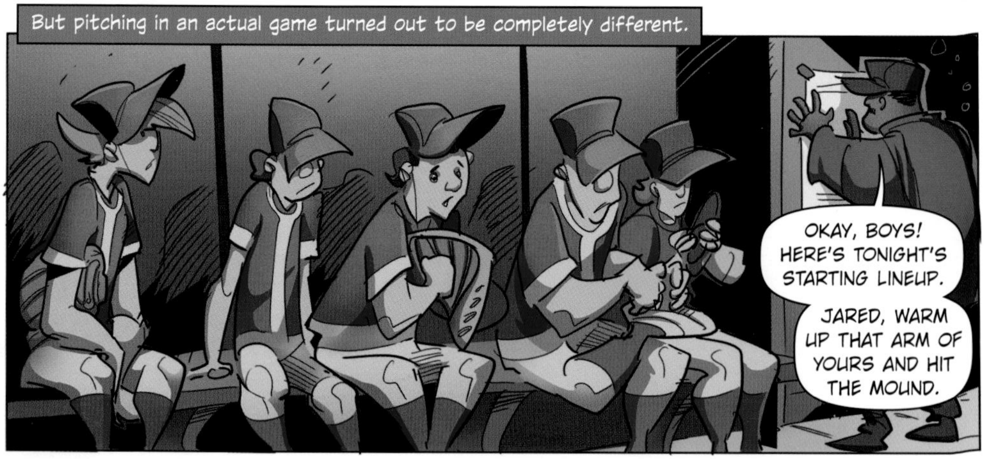
But pitching in an actual game turned out to be completely different.
OKAY, BOYS! HERE'S TONIGHT'S STARTING LINEUP.
JARED, WARM UP THAT ARM OF YOURS AND HIT THE MOUND.

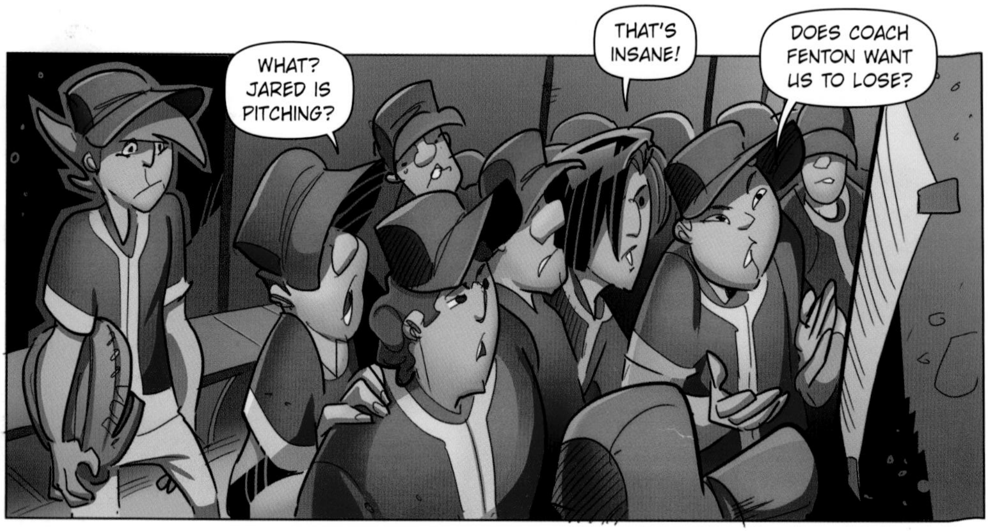
WHAT? JARED IS PITCHING?
THAT'S INSANE!
DOES COACH FENTON WANT US TO LOSE?

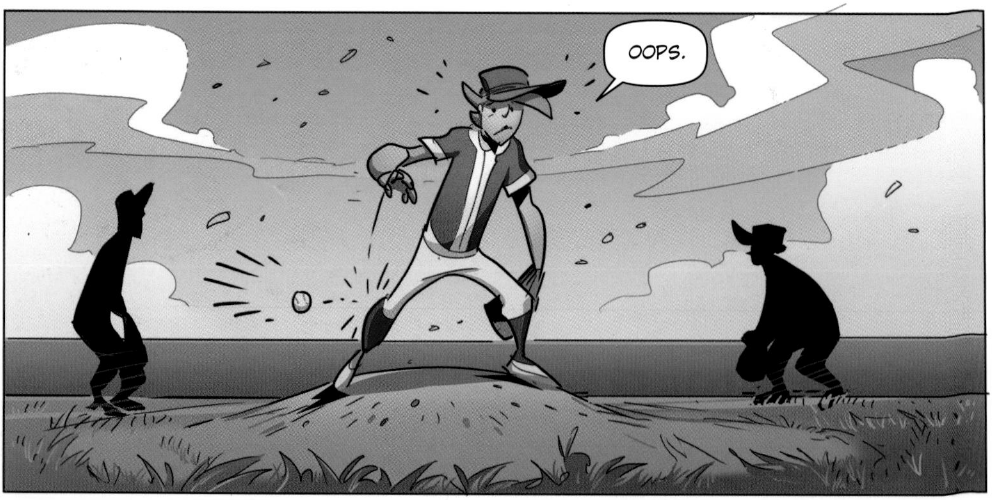
OOPS.

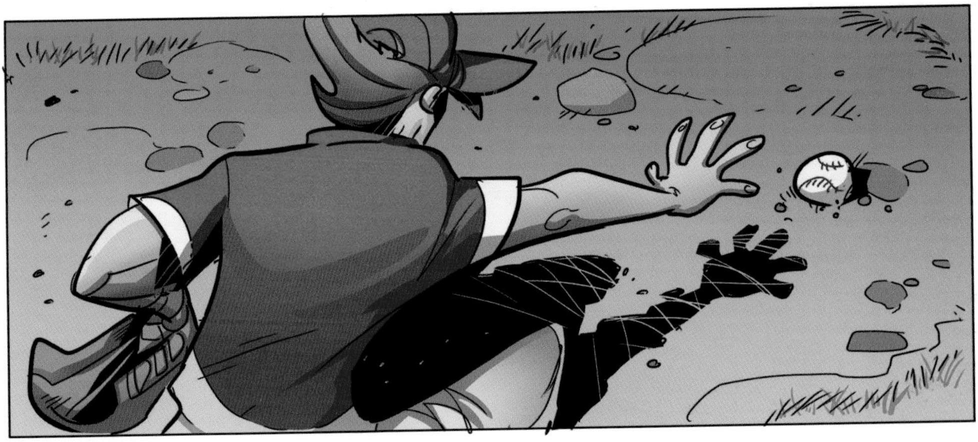

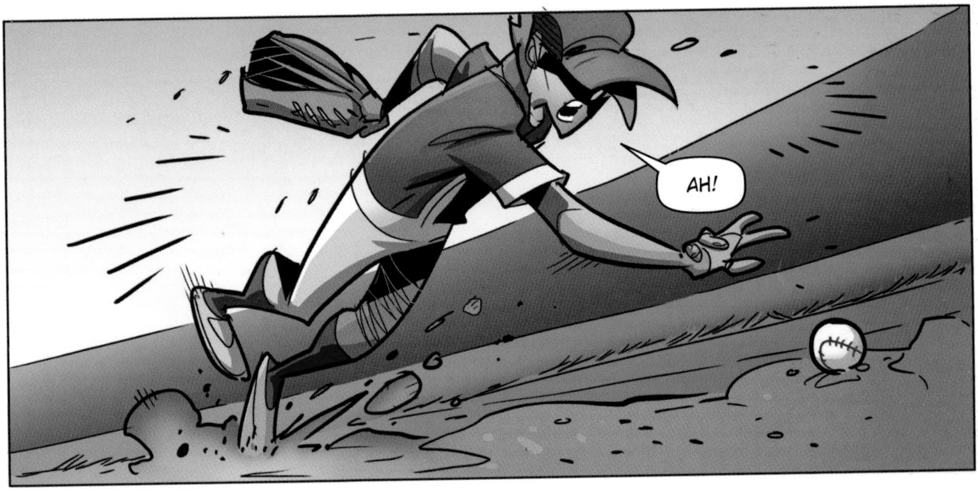
AH!

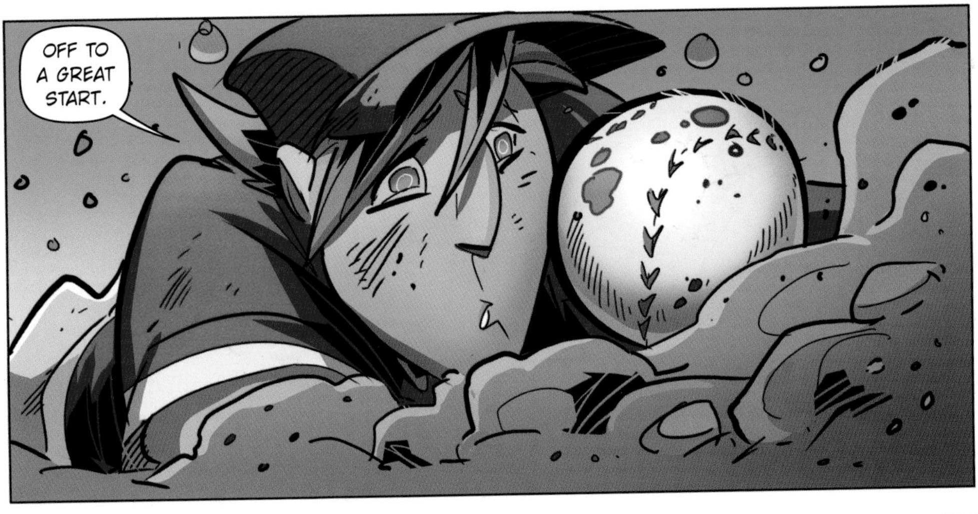
OFF TO A GREAT START.

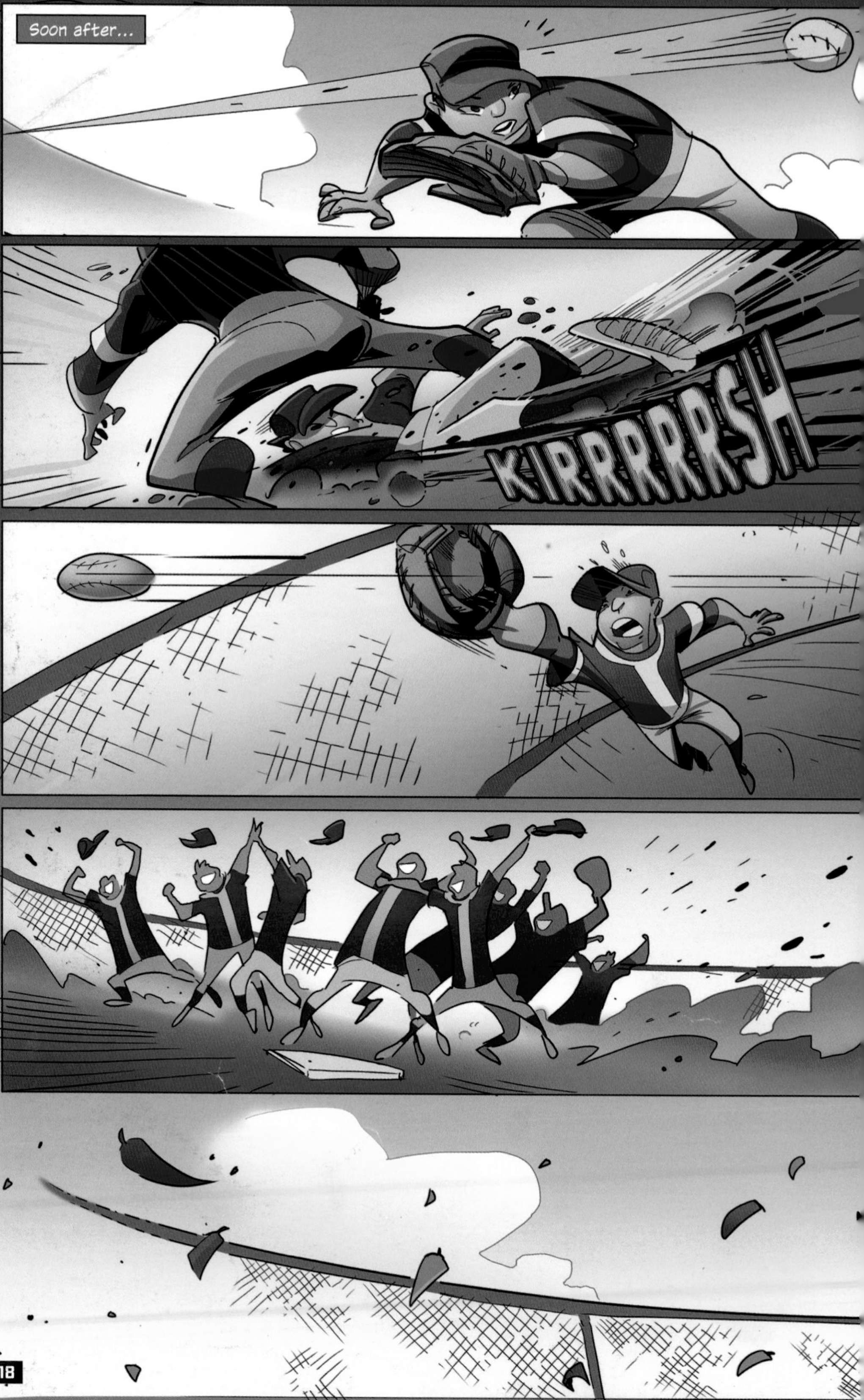
Soon after...
KIRRRRRRSH

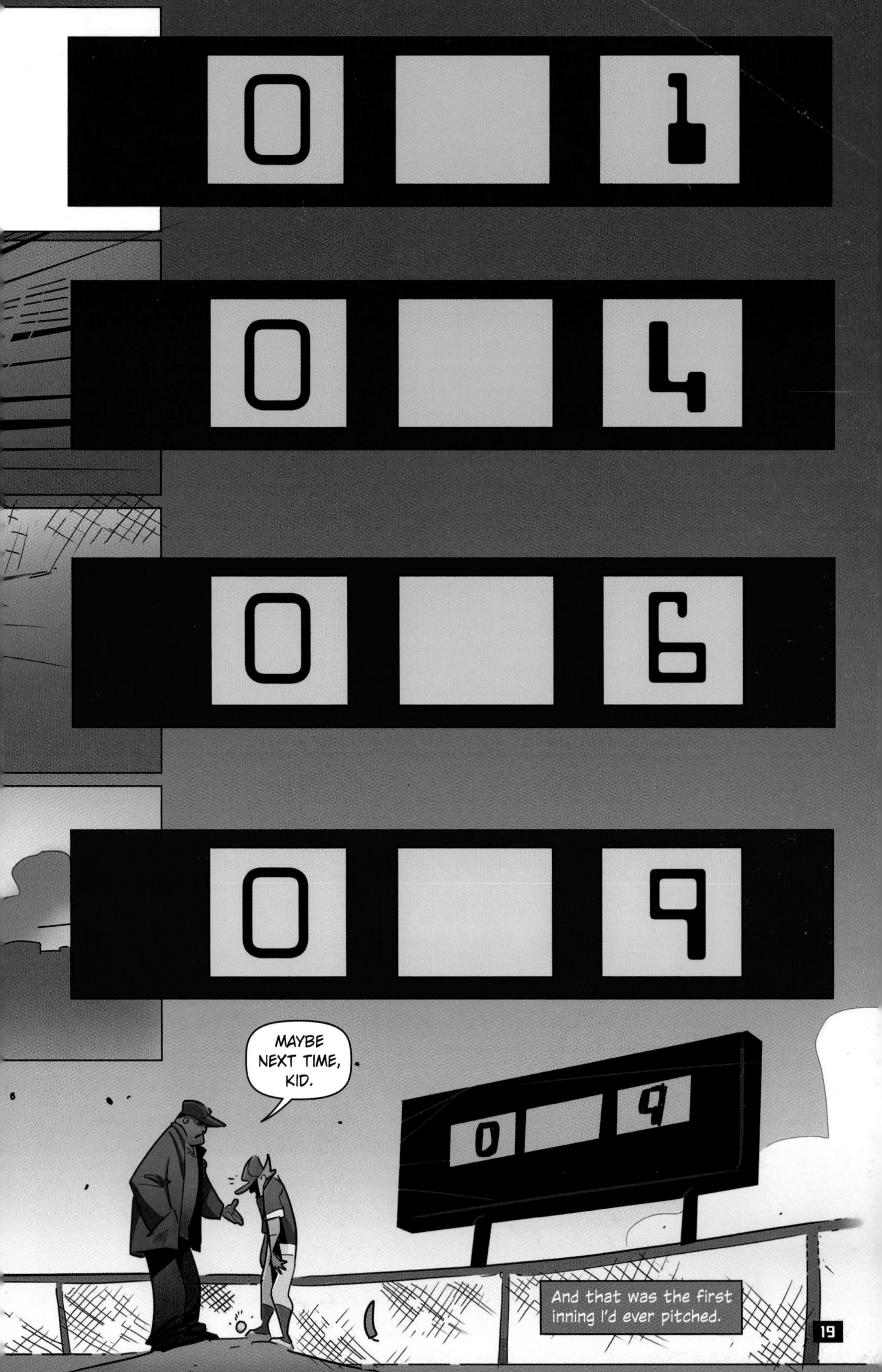
0 1
0 4
0 6
0 9
MAYBE NEXT TIME, KID.
0 9
And that was the first inning I'd ever pitched.

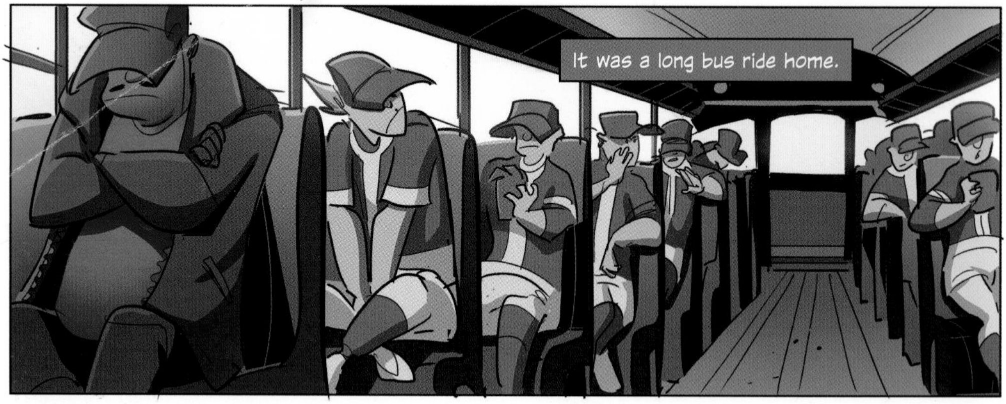
It was a long bus ride home.

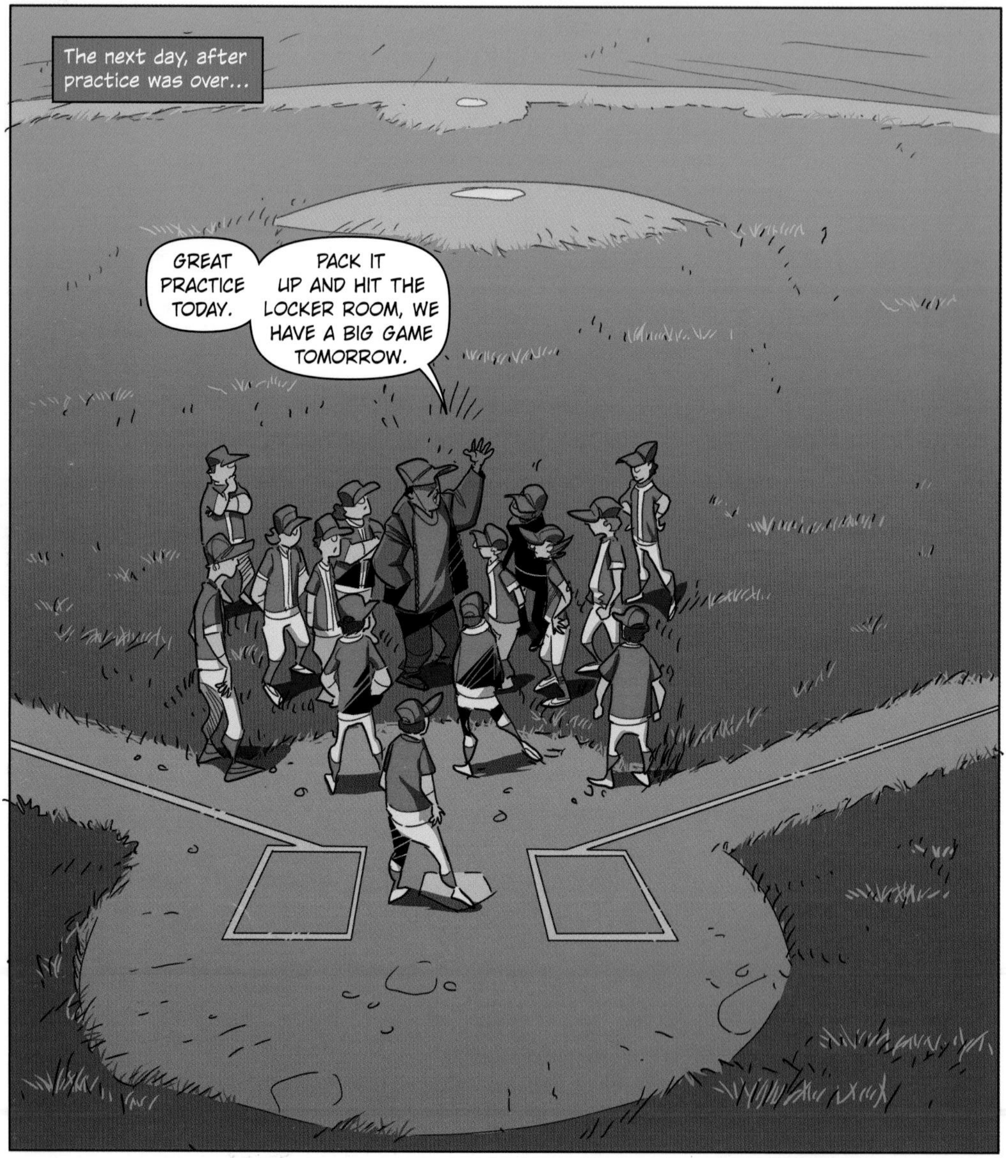
The next day, after practice was over...
GREAT PRACTICE TODAY.
PACK IT UP AND HIT THE LOCKER ROOM, WE HAVE A BIG GAME TOMORROW.

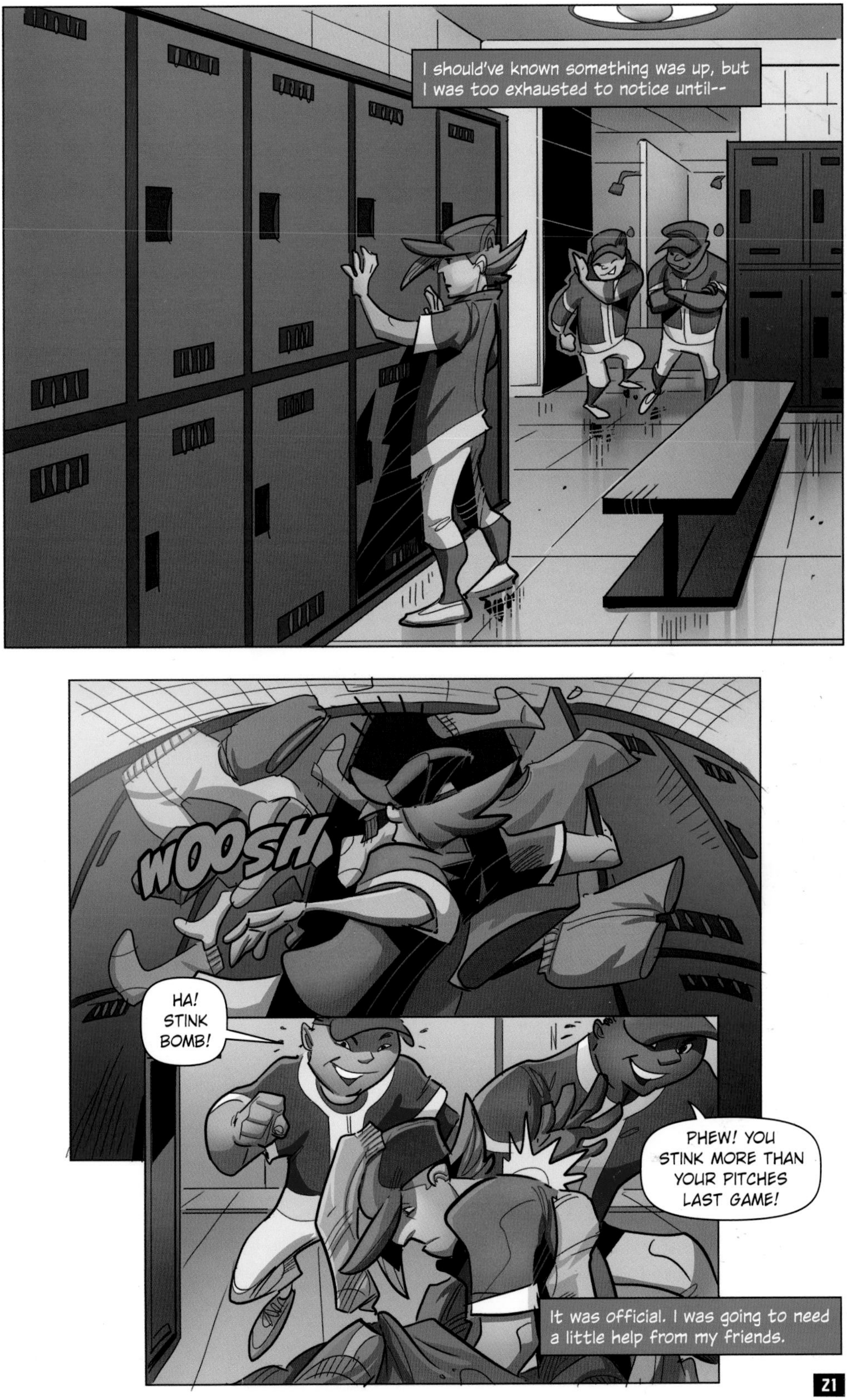
I should've known something was up, but I was too exhausted to notice until--
WOOSH
HA! STINK BOMB!
PHEW! YOU STINK MORE THAN YOUR PITCHES LAST GAME!
It was official. I was going to need a little help from my friends.

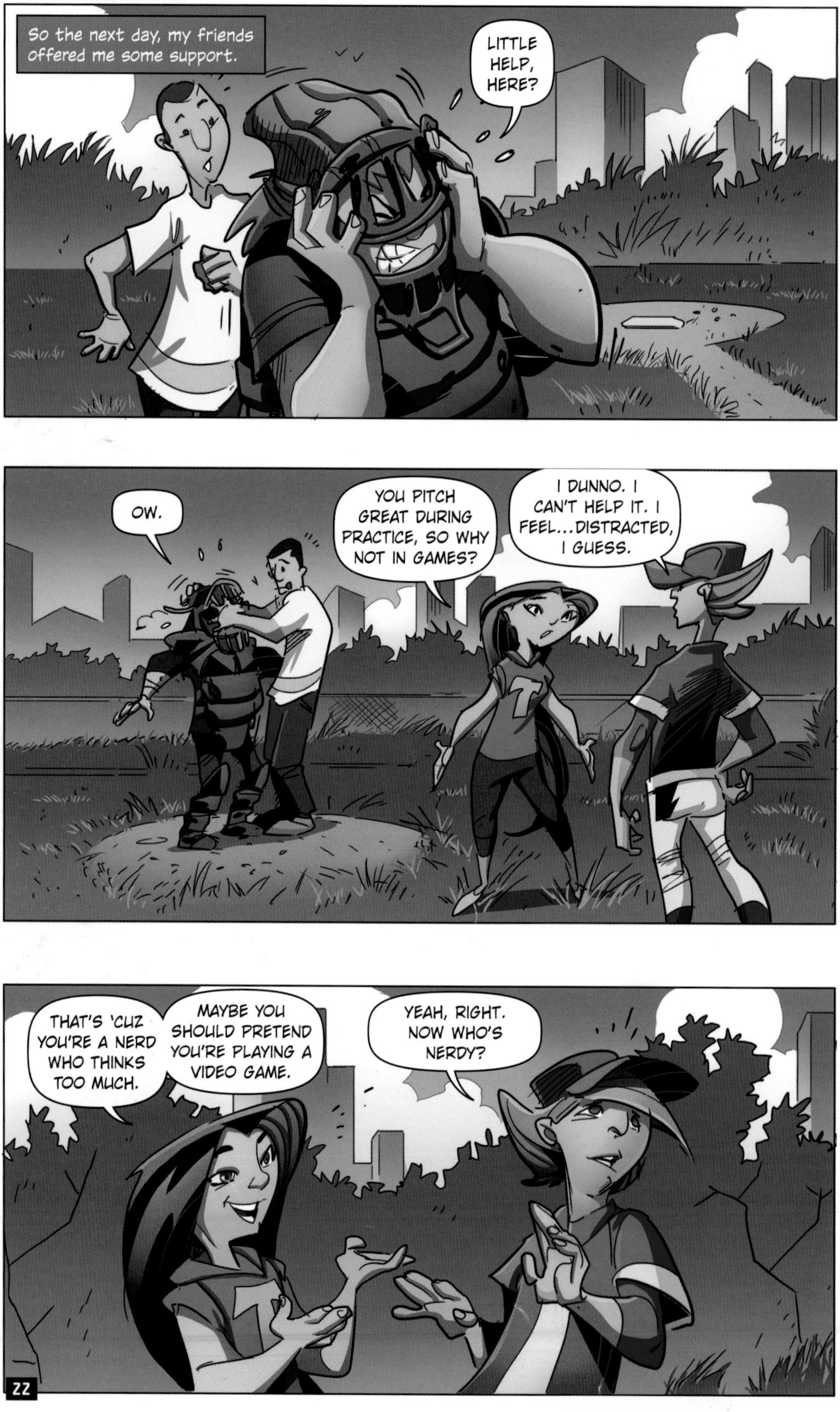
So the next day, my friends offered me some support.
LITTLE HELP, HERE?
OW.
YOU PITCH GREAT DURING PRACTICE, SO WHY NOT IN GAMES?
I DUNNO. I CAN'T HELP IT. I FEEL...DISTRACTED, I GUESS.
THAT'S 'CUZ YOU'RE A NERD WHO THINKS TOO MUCH.
MAYBE YOU SHOULD PRETEND YOU'RE PLAYING A VIDEO GAME.
YEAH, RIGHT. NOW WHO'S NERDY?

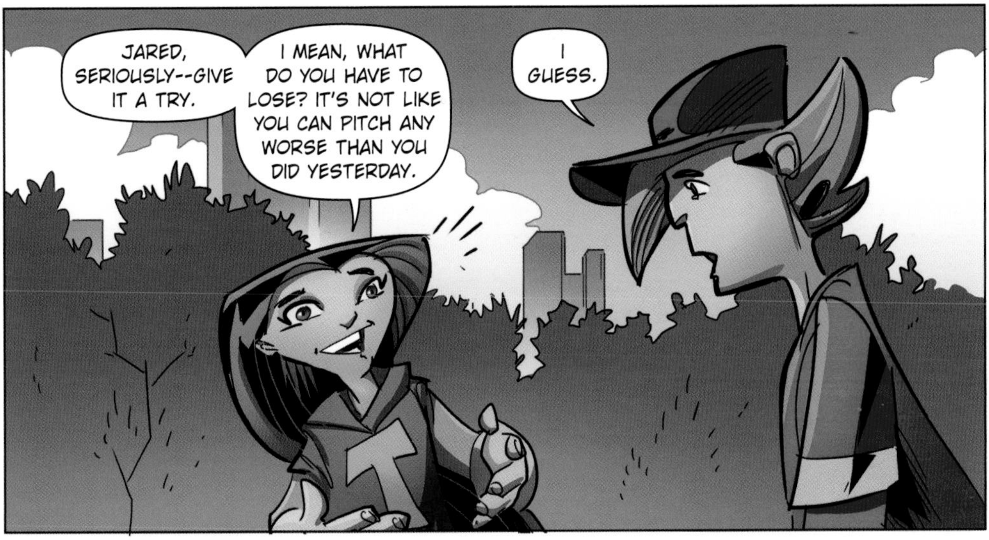
JARED, SERIOUSLY--GIVE IT A TRY.
I MEAN, WHAT DO YOU HAVE TO LOSE? IT'S NOT LIKE YOU CAN PITCH ANY WORSE THAN YOU DID YESTERDAY.
I GUESS.

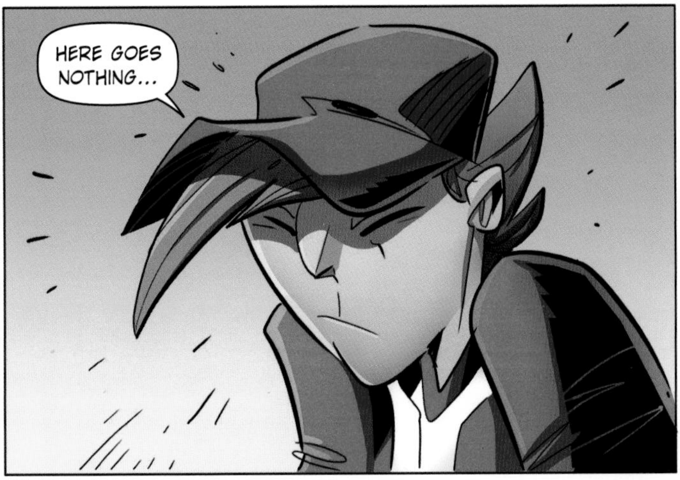
HERE GOES NOTHING...

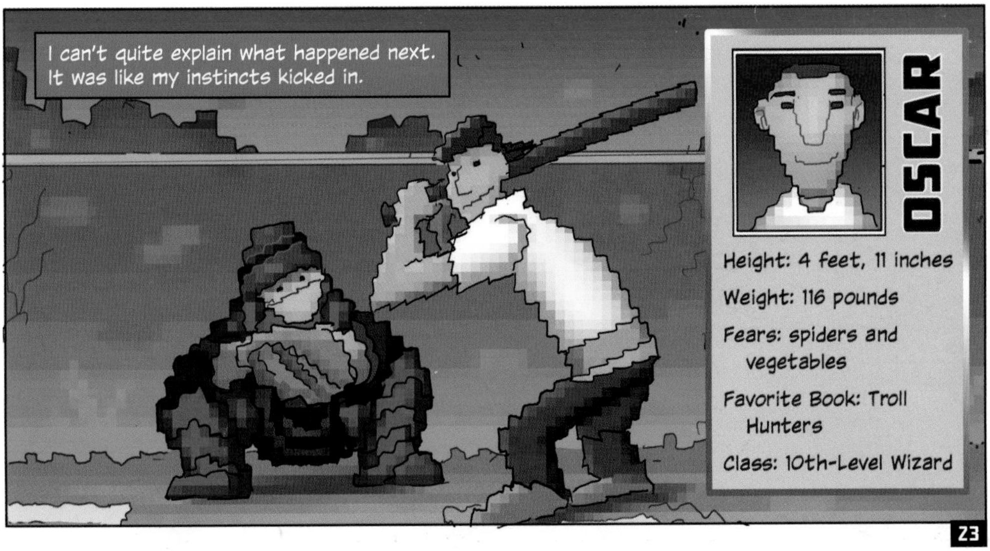
I can't quite explain what happened next. It was like my instincts kicked in.
OSCAR
Height: 4 feet, 11 inches
Weight: 116 pounds
Fears: spiders and vegetables
Favorite Book: Troll Hunters
Class: 10th-Level Wizard

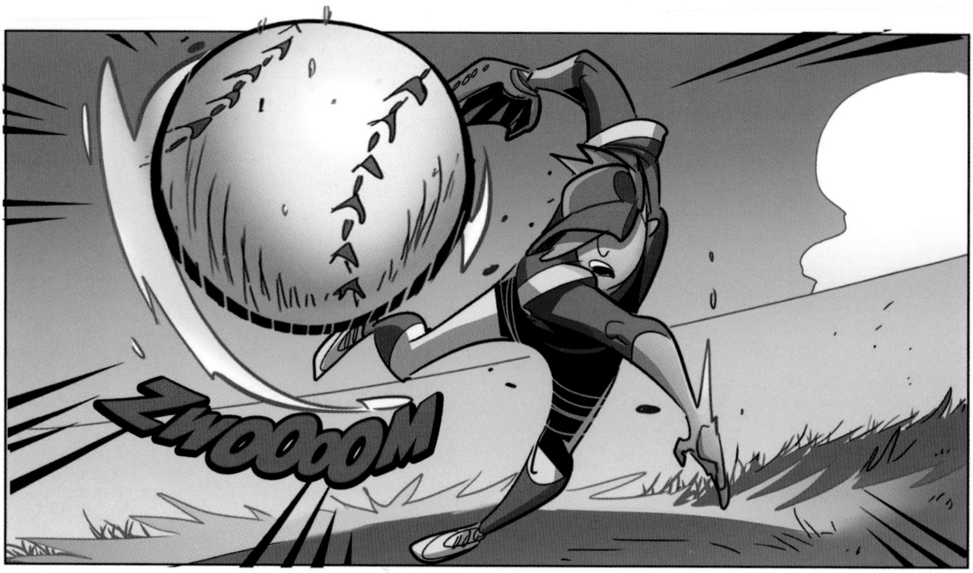
ZWOOOOOM

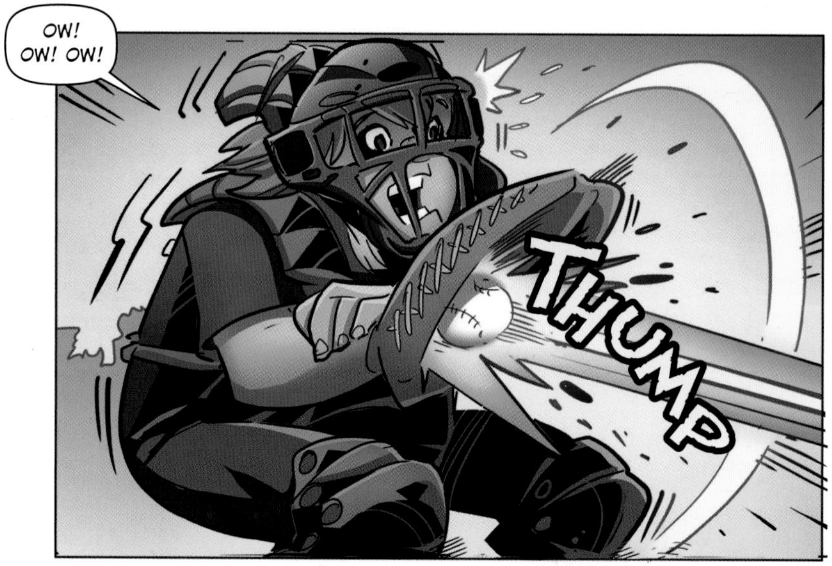
OW! OW! OW!
THUMP

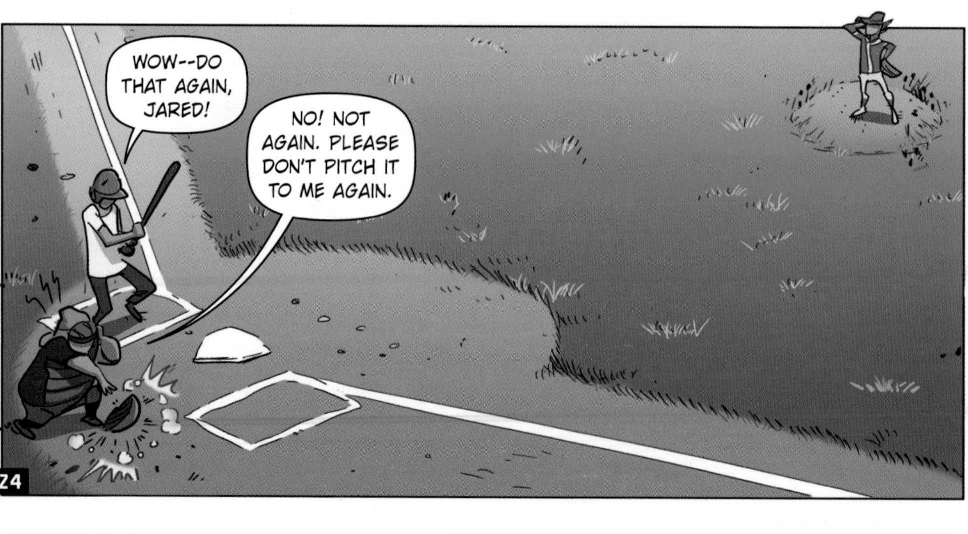
WOW--DO THAT AGAIN, JARED!
NO! NOT AGAIN. PLEASE DON'T PITCH IT TO ME AGAIN.

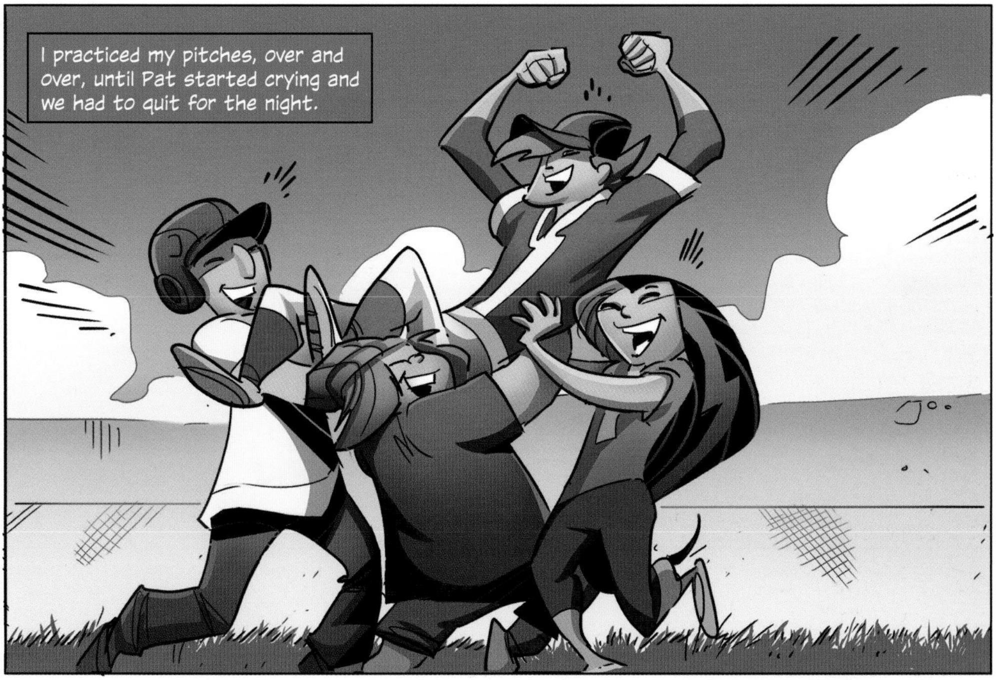
I practiced my pitches, over and over, until Pat started crying and we had to quit for the night.

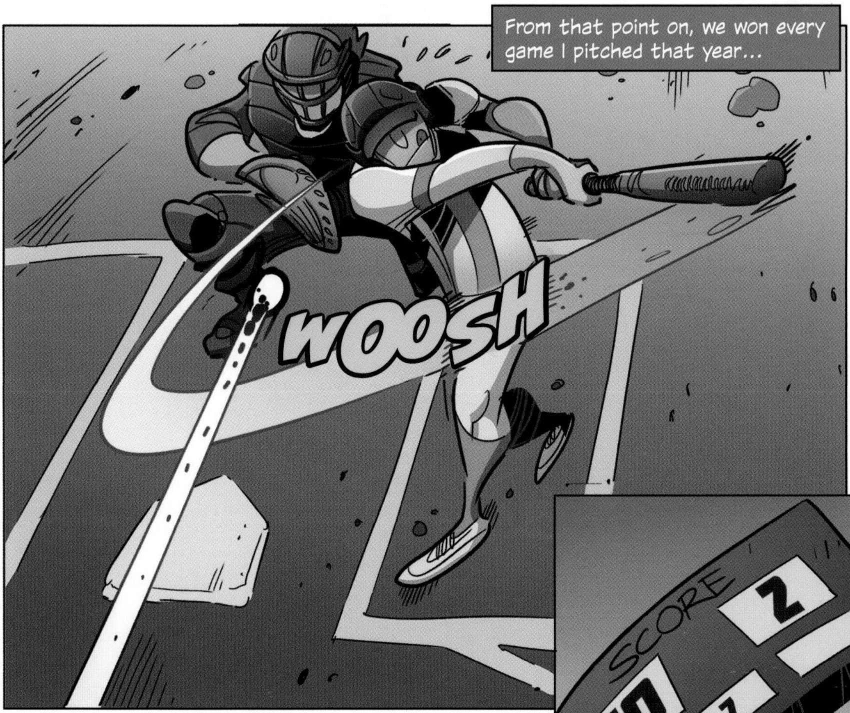
From that point on, we won every game I pitched that year...
WOOSH

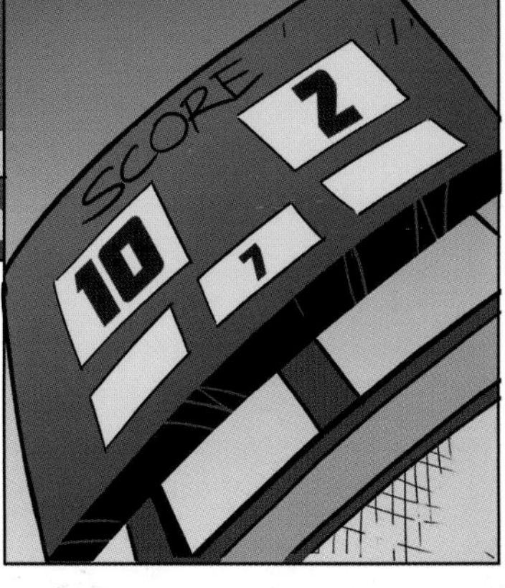
SCORE
2
10
7

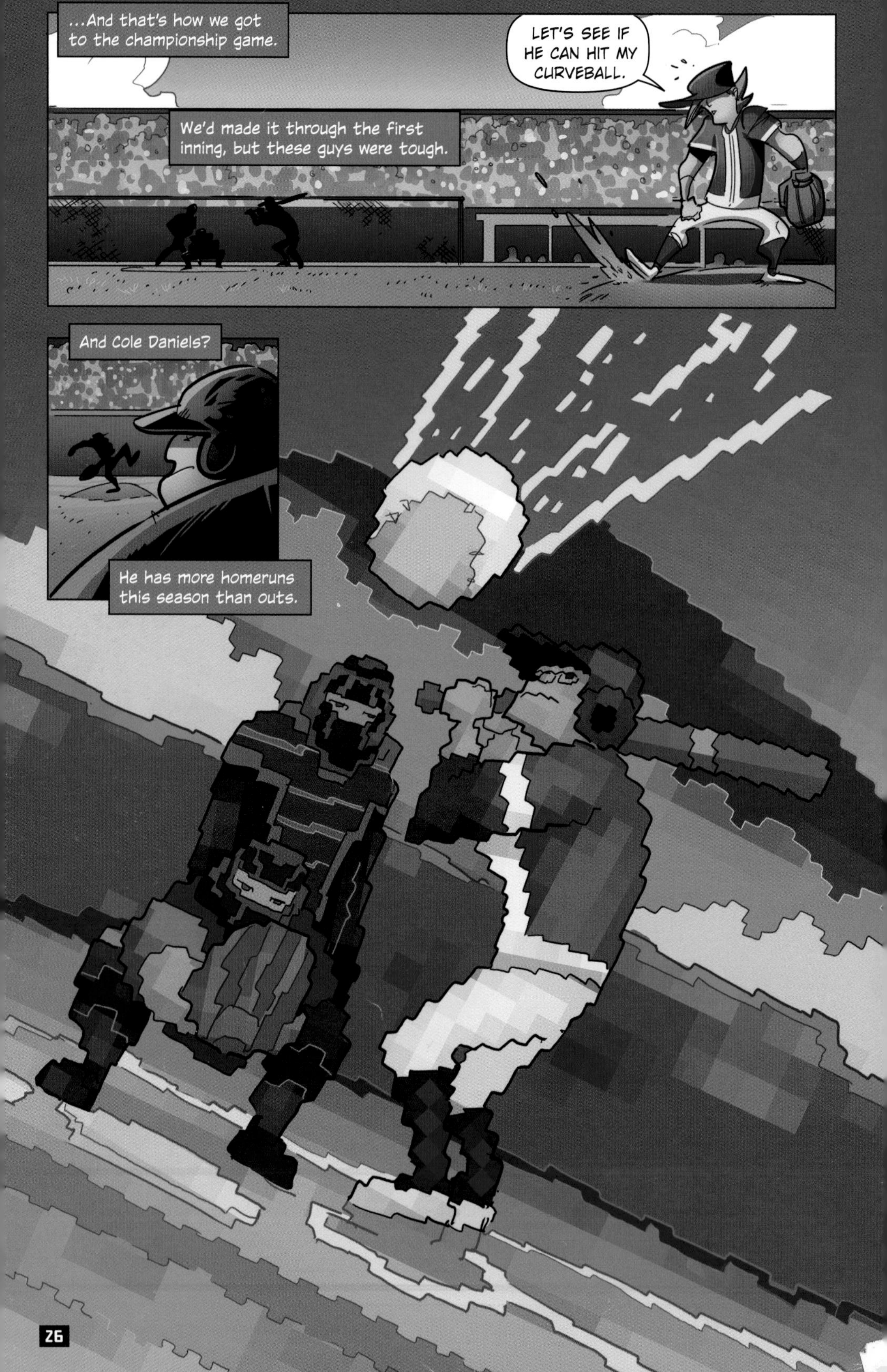
...And that's how we got to the championship game.
LET'S SEE IF HE CAN HIT MY CURVEBALL.
We'd made it through the first inning, but these guys were tough.
And Cole Daniels?
He has more homeruns this season than outs.

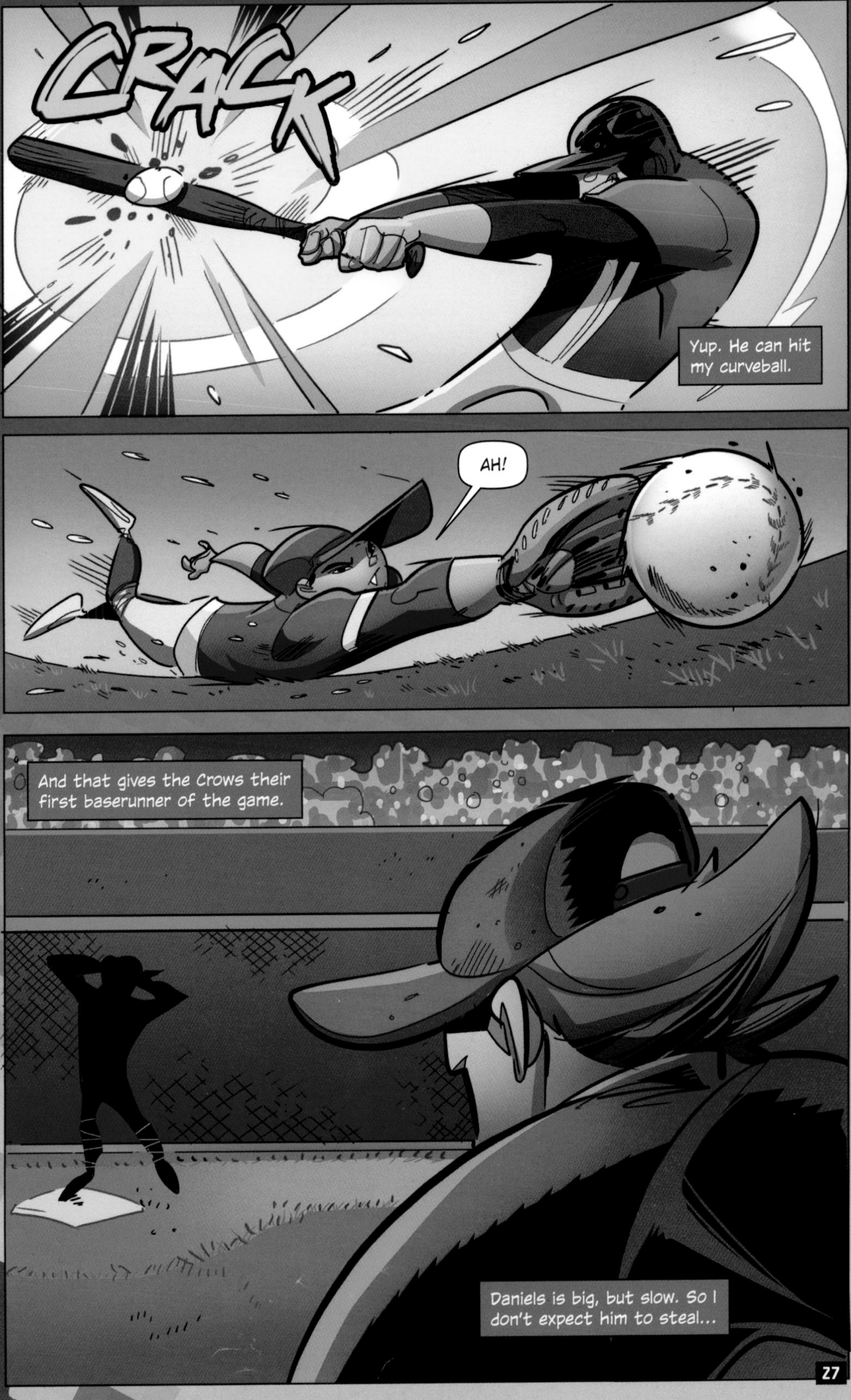
CRACK
Yup. He can hit my curveball.
AH!
And that gives the Crows their first baserunner of the game.
Daniels is big, but slow. So I don't expect him to steal...

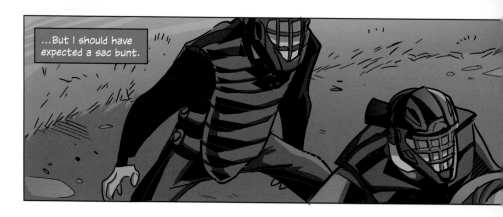

...But I should have expected a sac bunt.

OUT

On the next pitch...

CRACK

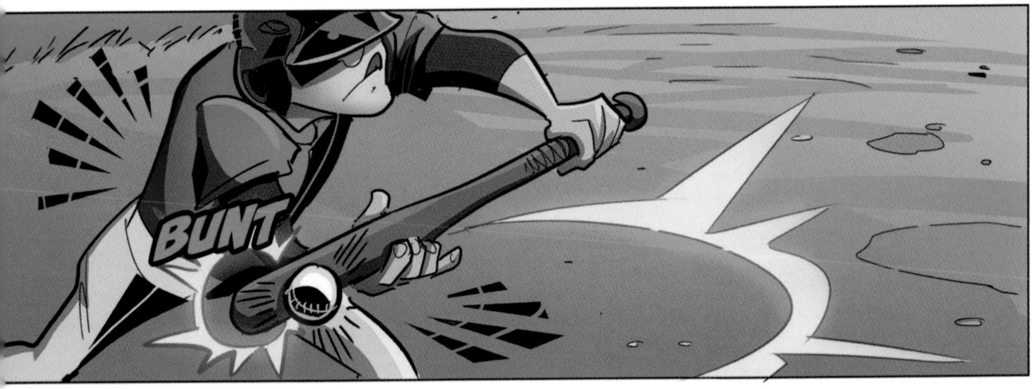
BUNT

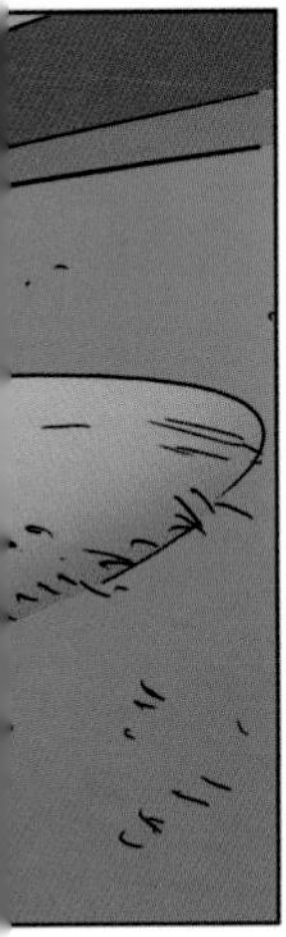

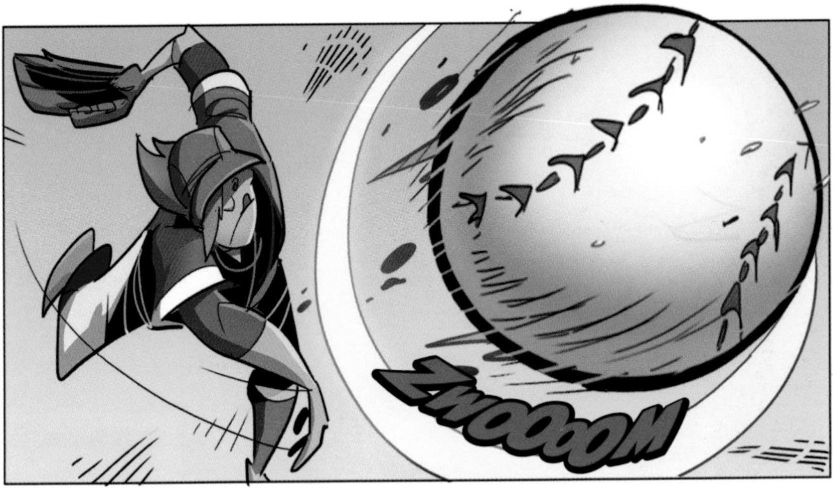
ZWOOOOM

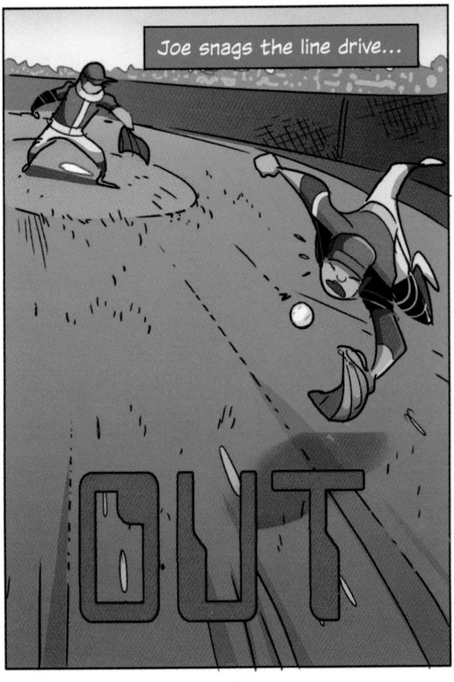
Joe snags the line drive...
OUT

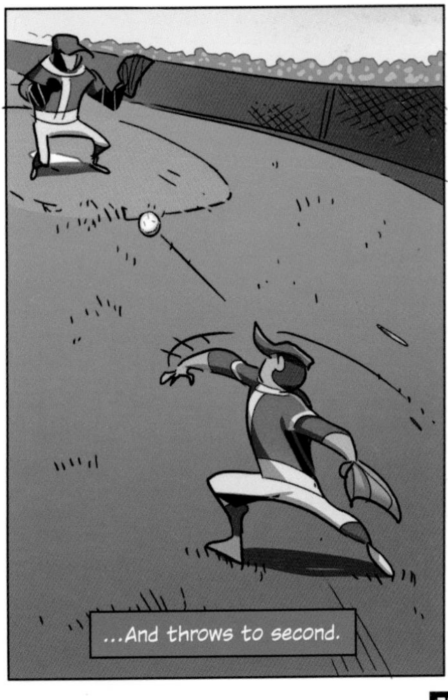
...And throws to second.

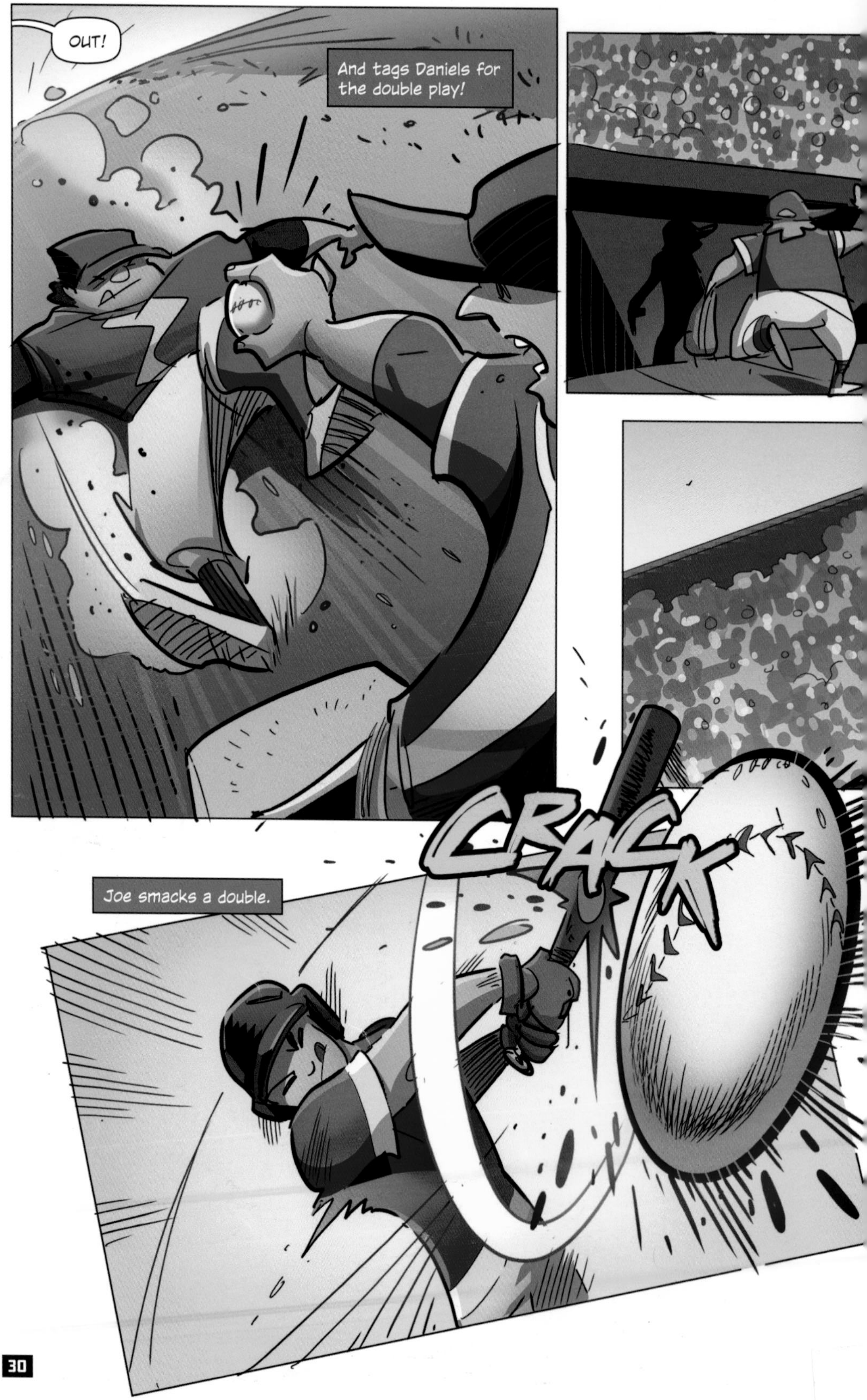
OUT!
And tags Daniels for the double play!
Joe smacks a double.
CRACK

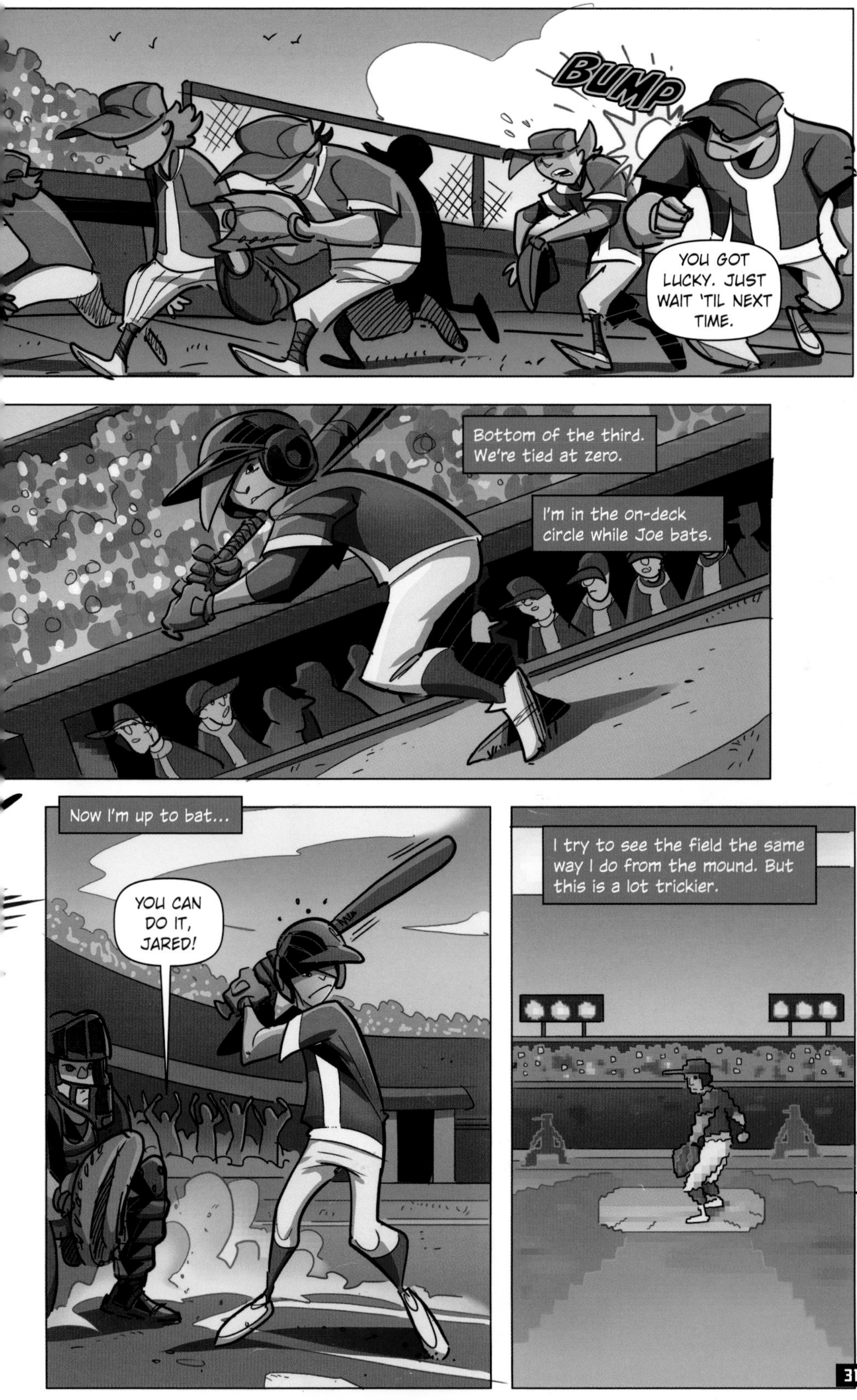
BUMP
YOU GOT LUCKY. JUST WAIT 'TIL NEXT TIME.
Bottom of the third. We're tied at zero.
I'm in the on-deck circle while Joe bats.
Now I'm up to bat...
YOU CAN DO IT, JARED!
I try to see the field the same way I do from the mound. But this is a lot trickier.

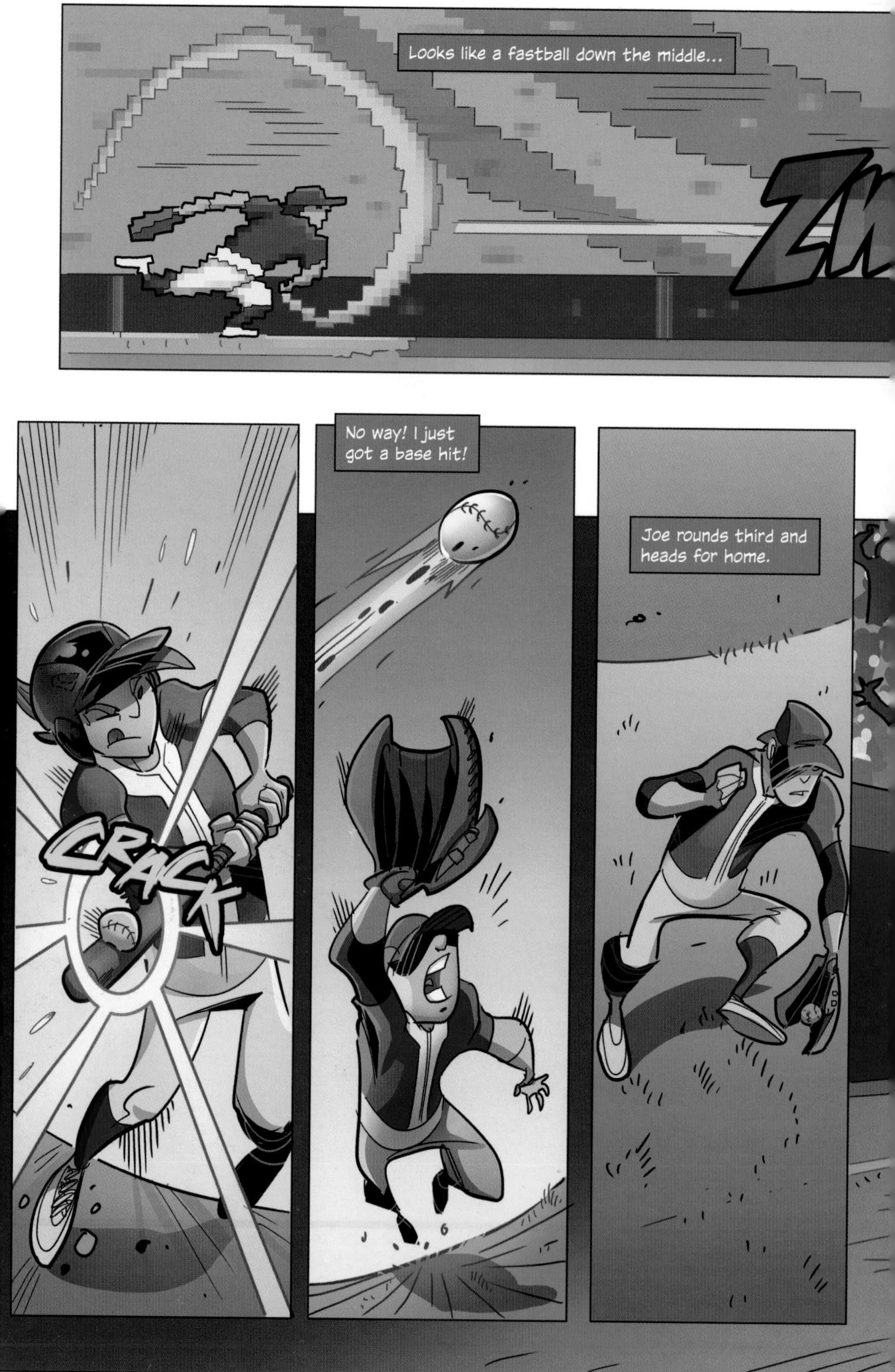
Looks like a fastball down the middle...
ZW
CRACK
No way! I just got a base hit!
Joe rounds third and heads for home.

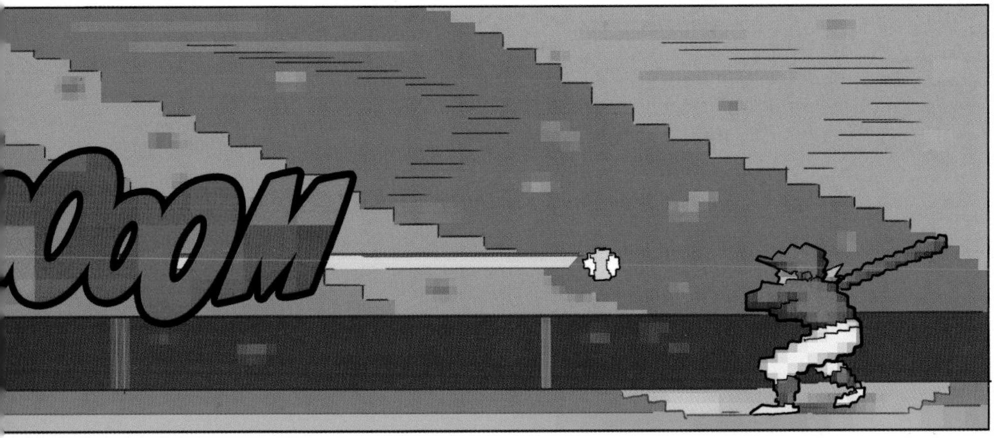
OOOM

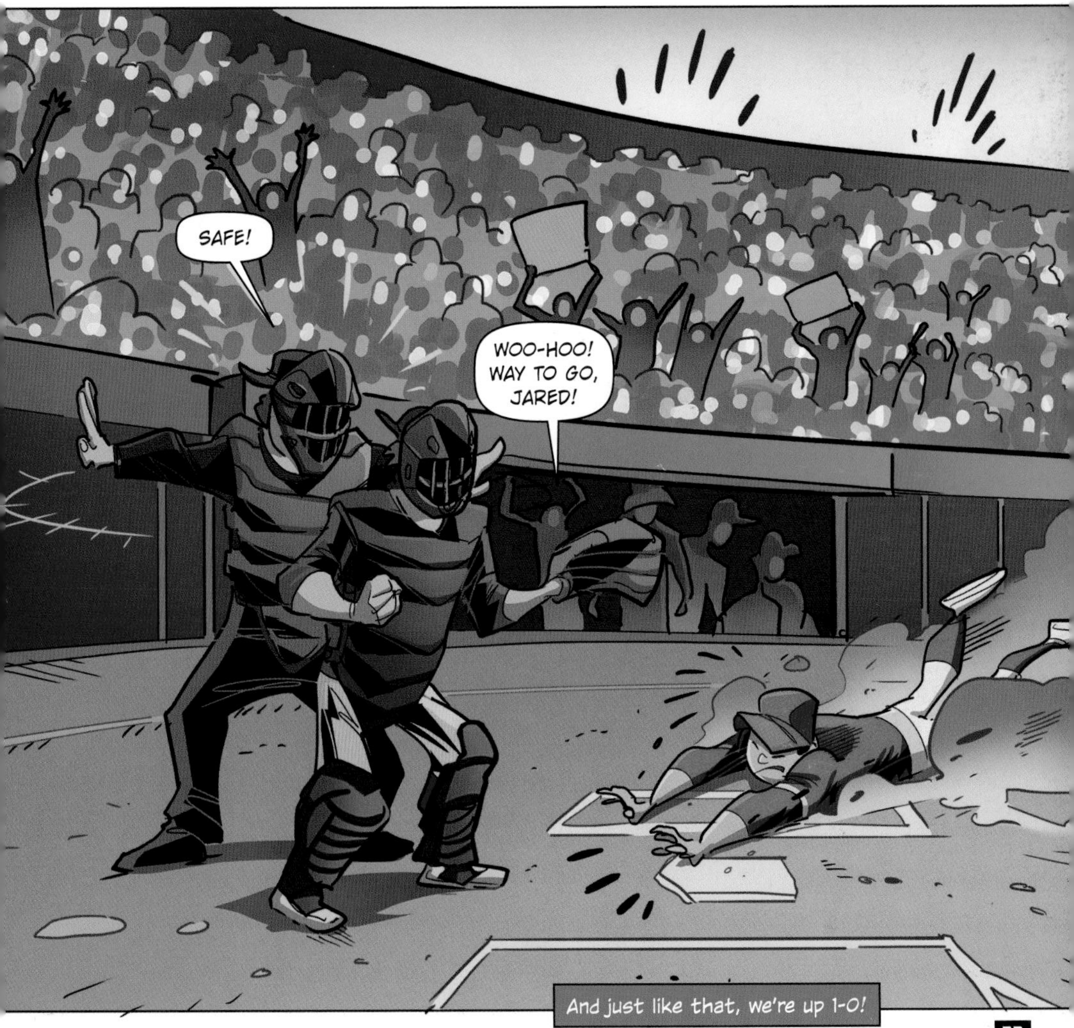
SAFE!
WOO-HOO! WAY TO GO, JARED!
And just like that, we're up 1-0!

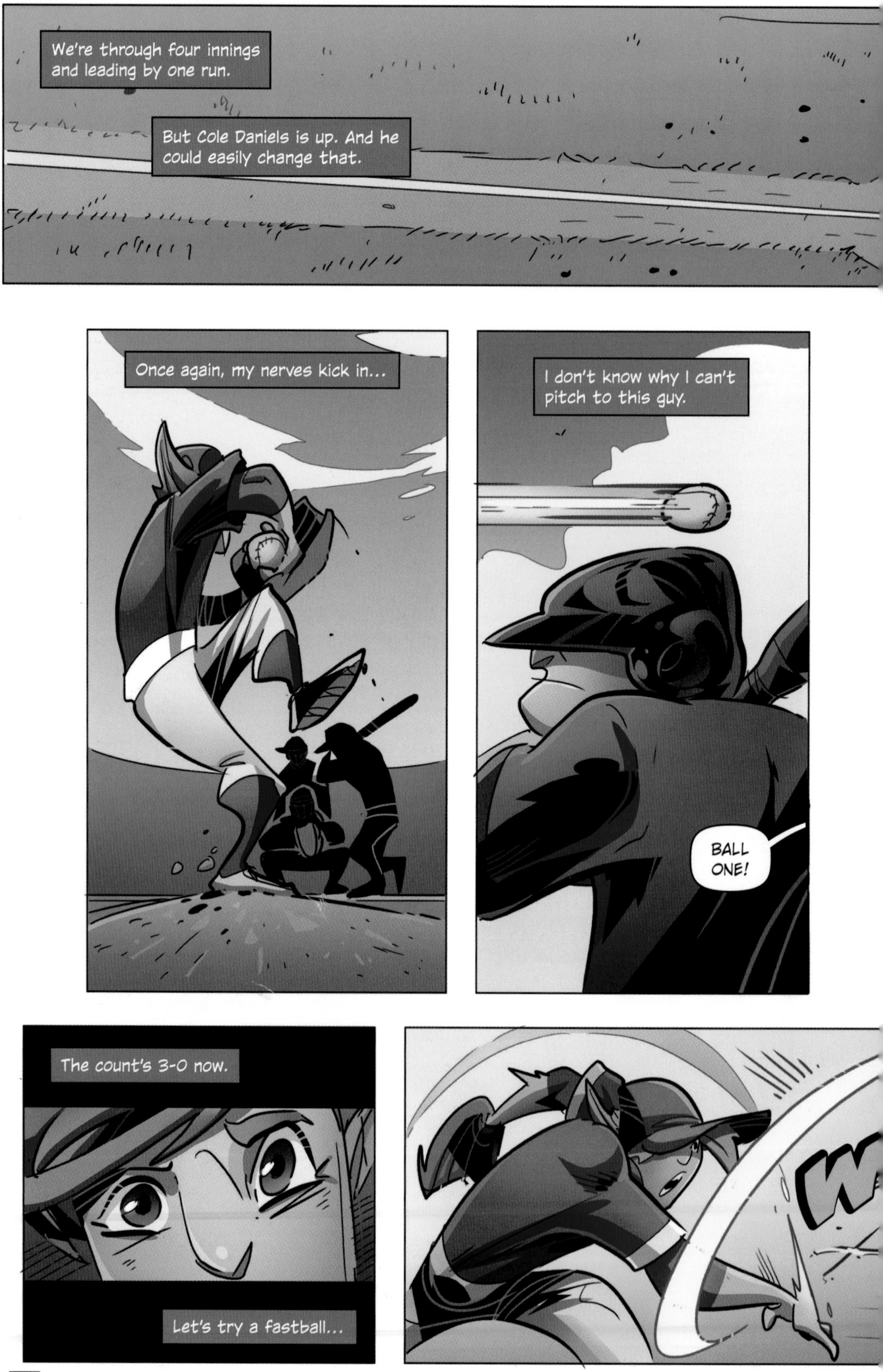
We're through four innings and leading by one run.
But Cole Daniels is up. And he could easily change that.
Once again, my nerves kick in...
I don't know why I can't pitch to this guy.
BALL ONE!
The count's 3-0 now.
Let's try a fastball...

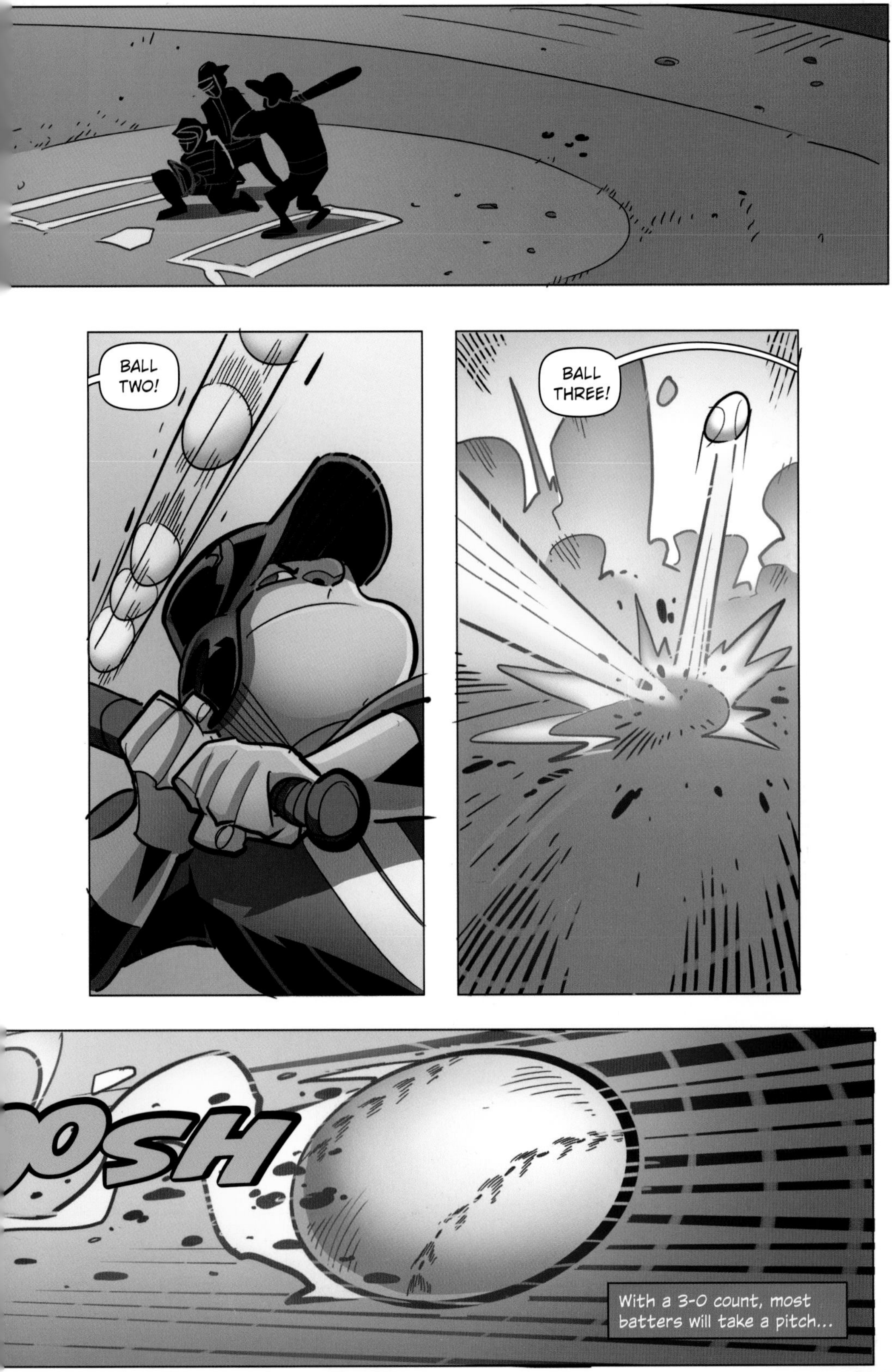
BALL TWO!
BALL THREE!
OOSH
With a 3-0 count, most batters will take a pitch...

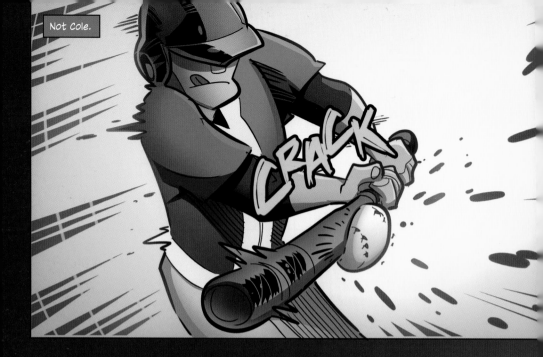

Not Cole.

CRACK

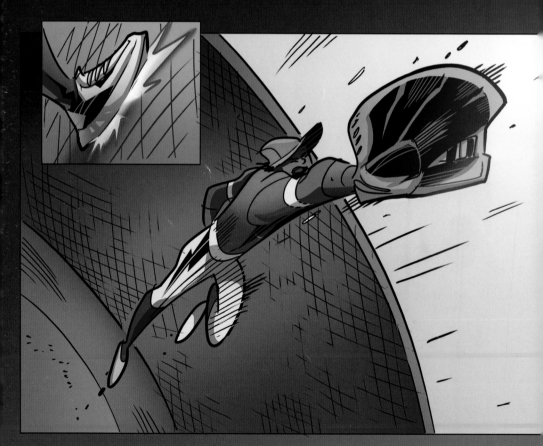

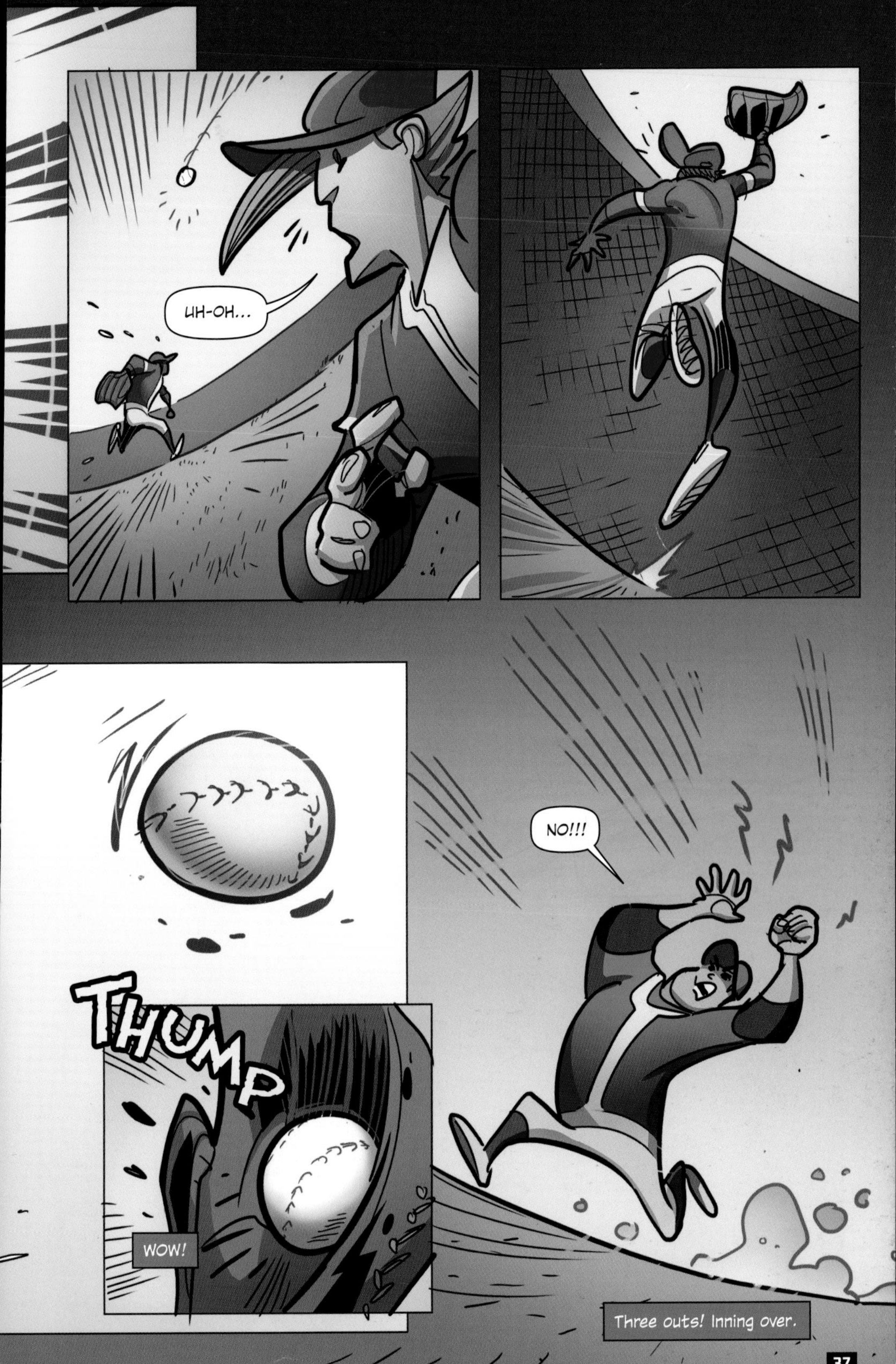
UH-OH...
NO!!!
THUMP
WOW!
Three outs! Inning over.

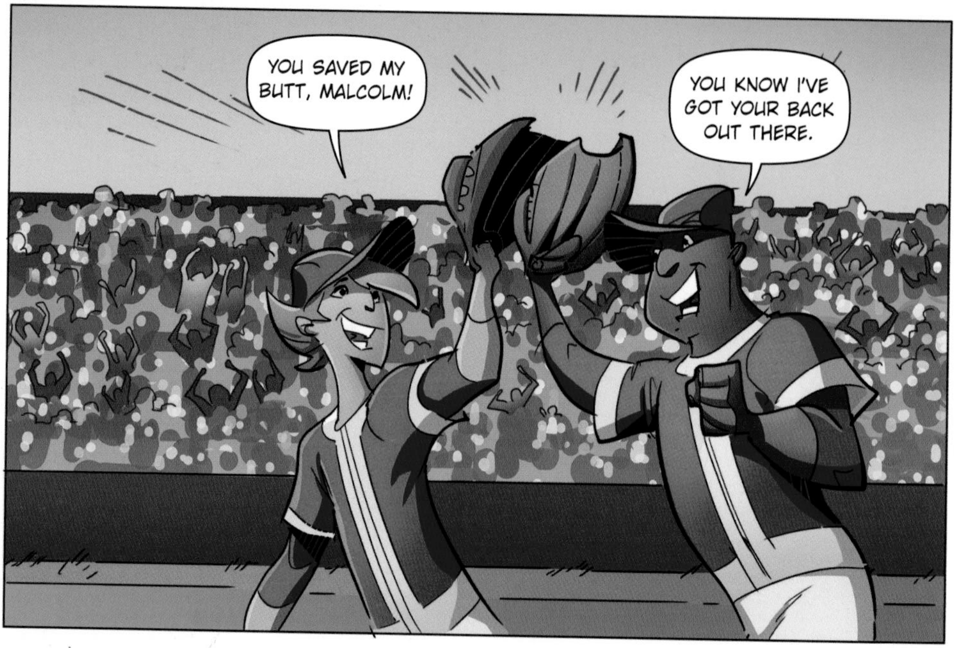
YOU SAVED MY BUTT, MALCOLM!
YOU KNOW I'VE GOT YOUR BACK OUT THERE.

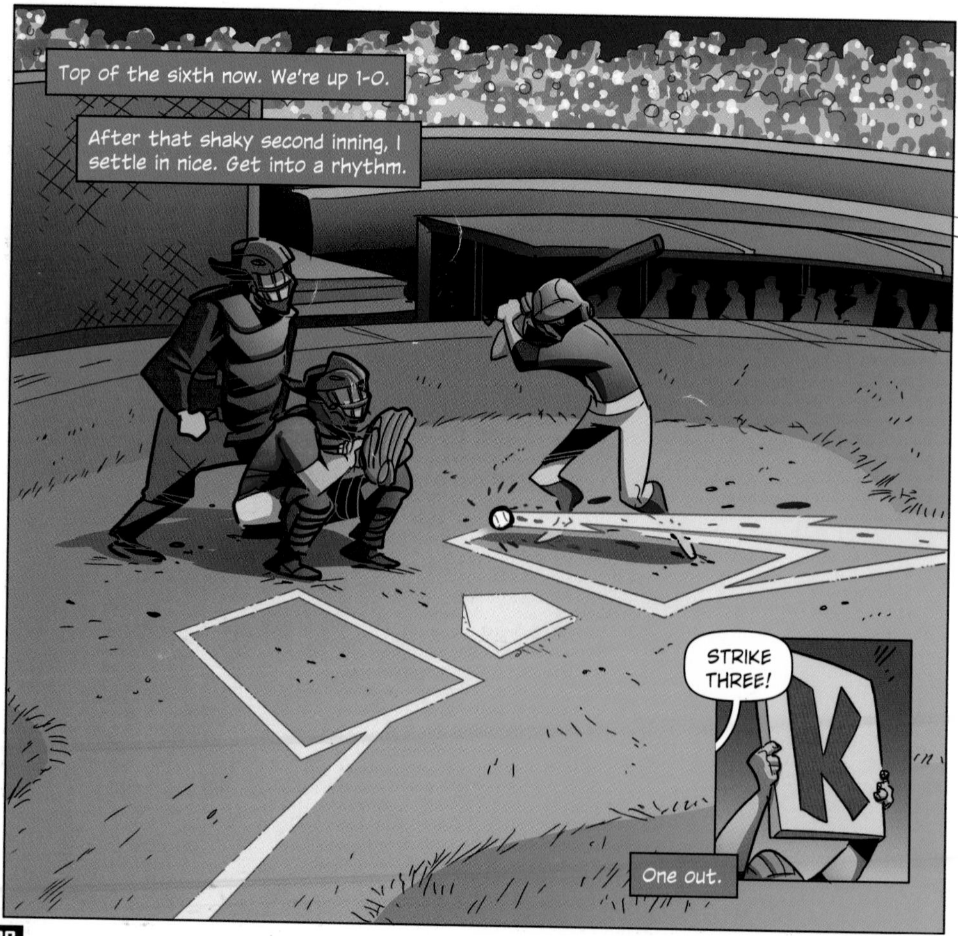
Top of the sixth now. We're up 1-0.
After that shaky second inning, I settle in nice. Get into a rhythm.
STRIKE THREE!
K
One out.

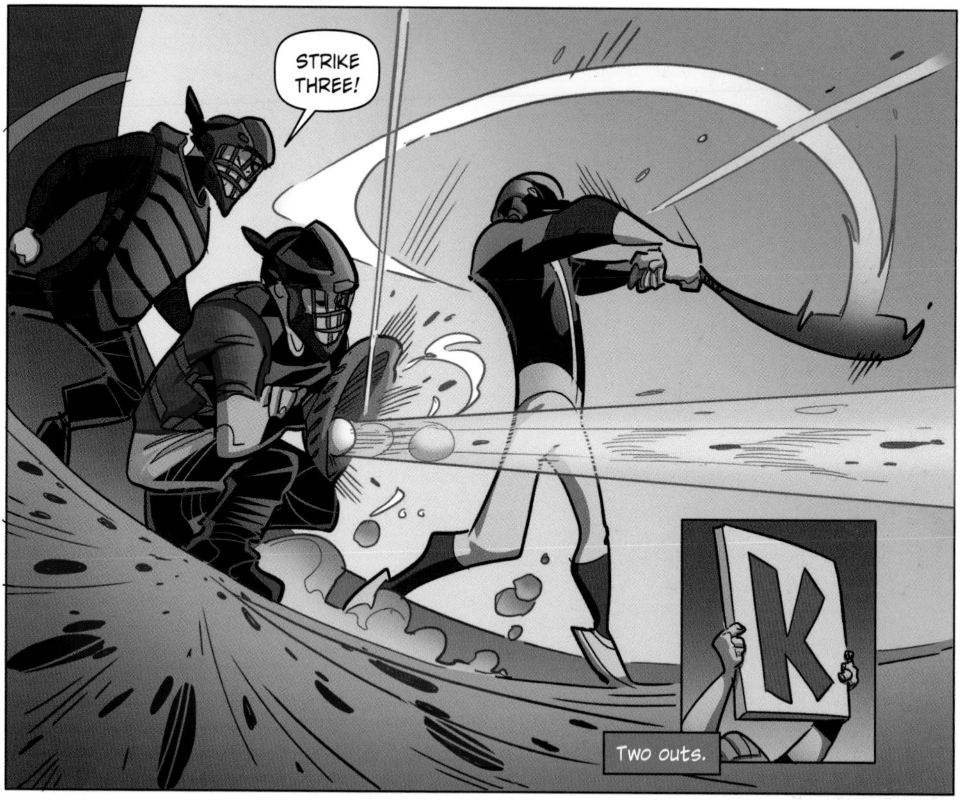
STRIKE THREE!
Two outs.

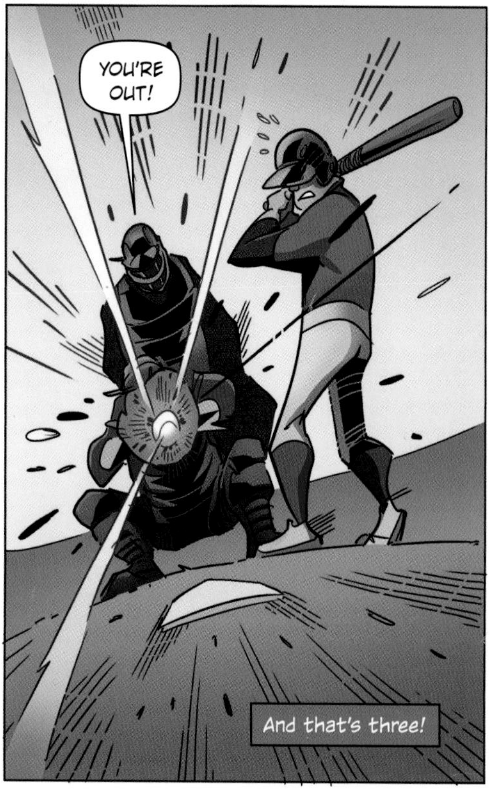
YOU'RE OUT!
And that's three!

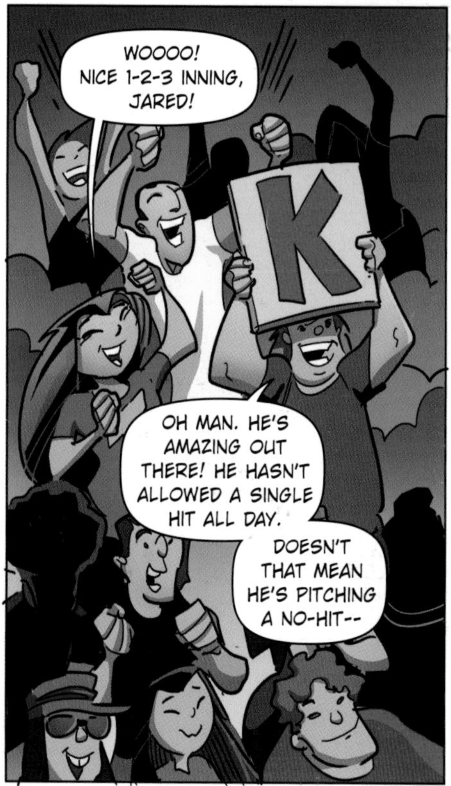
WOOOO! NICE 1-2-3 INNING, JARED!
OH MAN. HE'S AMAZING OUT THERE! HE HASN'T ALLOWED A SINGLE HIT ALL DAY.
DOESN'T THAT MEAN HE'S PITCHING A NO-HIT--

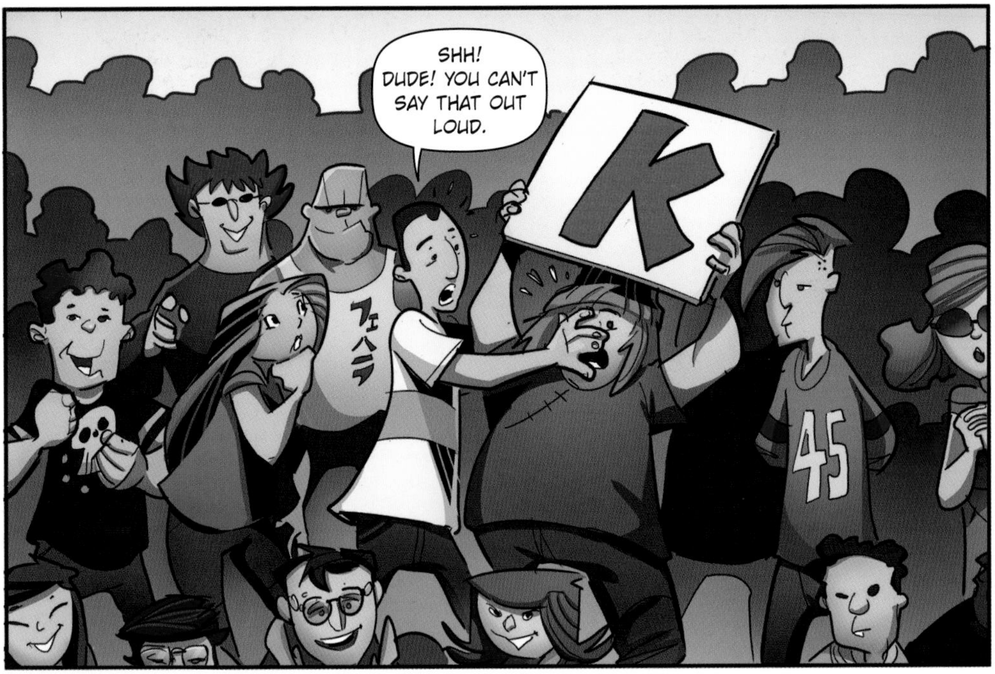
SHH! DUDE! YOU CAN'T SAY THAT OUT LOUD.
K

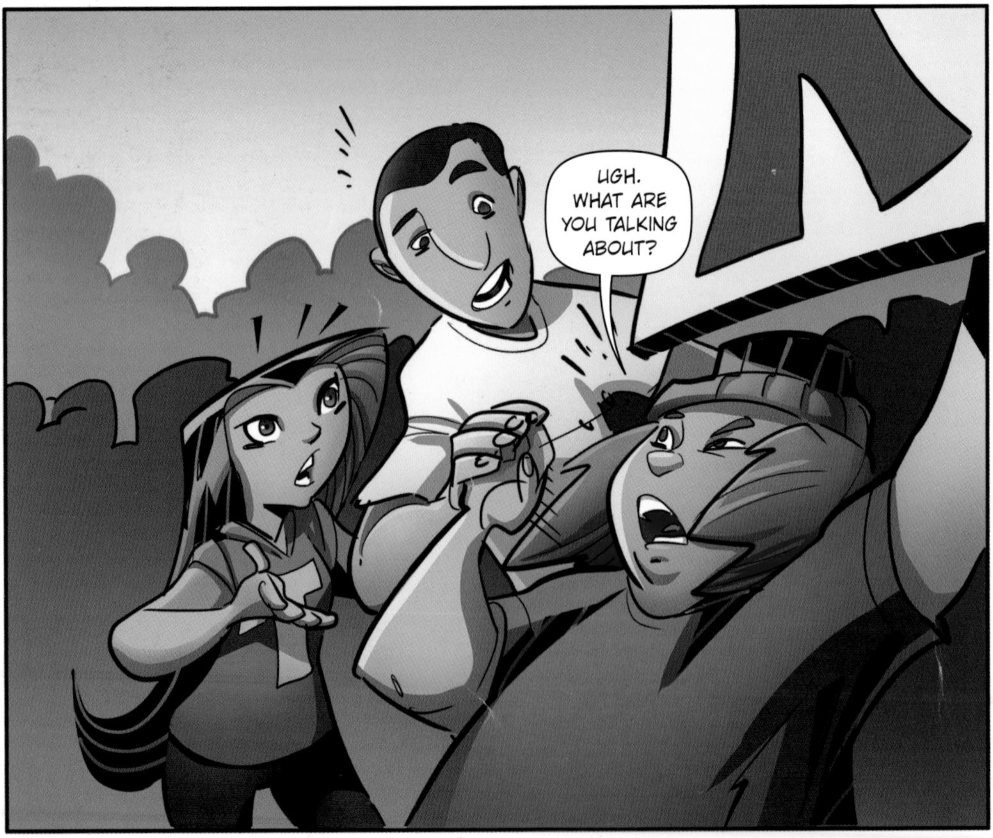
UGH. WHAT ARE YOU TALKING ABOUT?

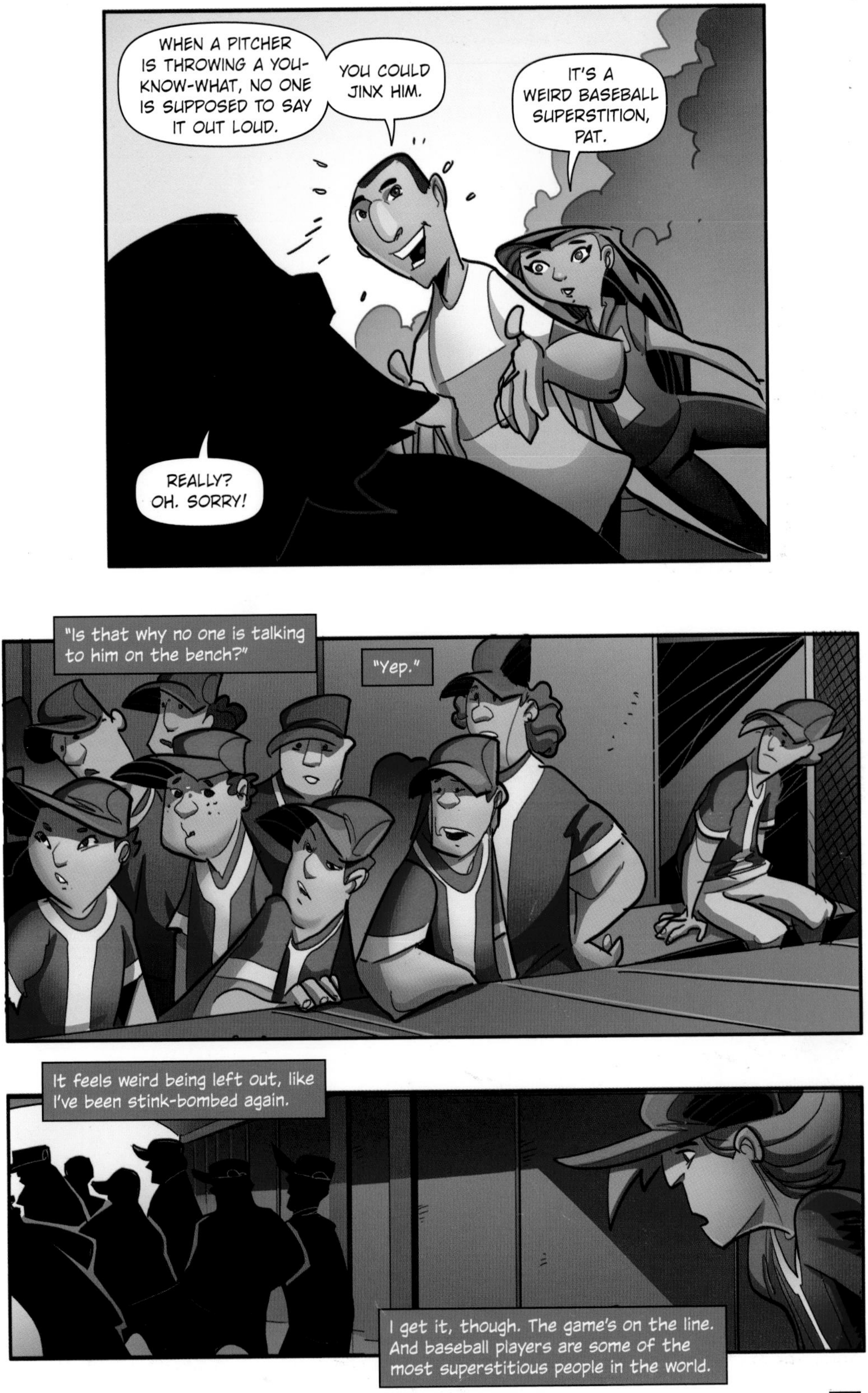
WHEN A PITCHER IS THROWING A YOU-KNOW-WHAT, NO ONE IS SUPPOSED TO SAY IT OUT LOUD.
YOU COULD JINX HIM.
IT'S A WEIRD BASEBALL SUPERSTITION, PAT.
REALLY? OH. SORRY!
"Is that why no one is talking to him on the bench?"
"Yep."
It feels weird being left out, like I've been stink-bombed again.
I get it, though. The game's on the line. And baseball players are some of the most superstitious people in the world.

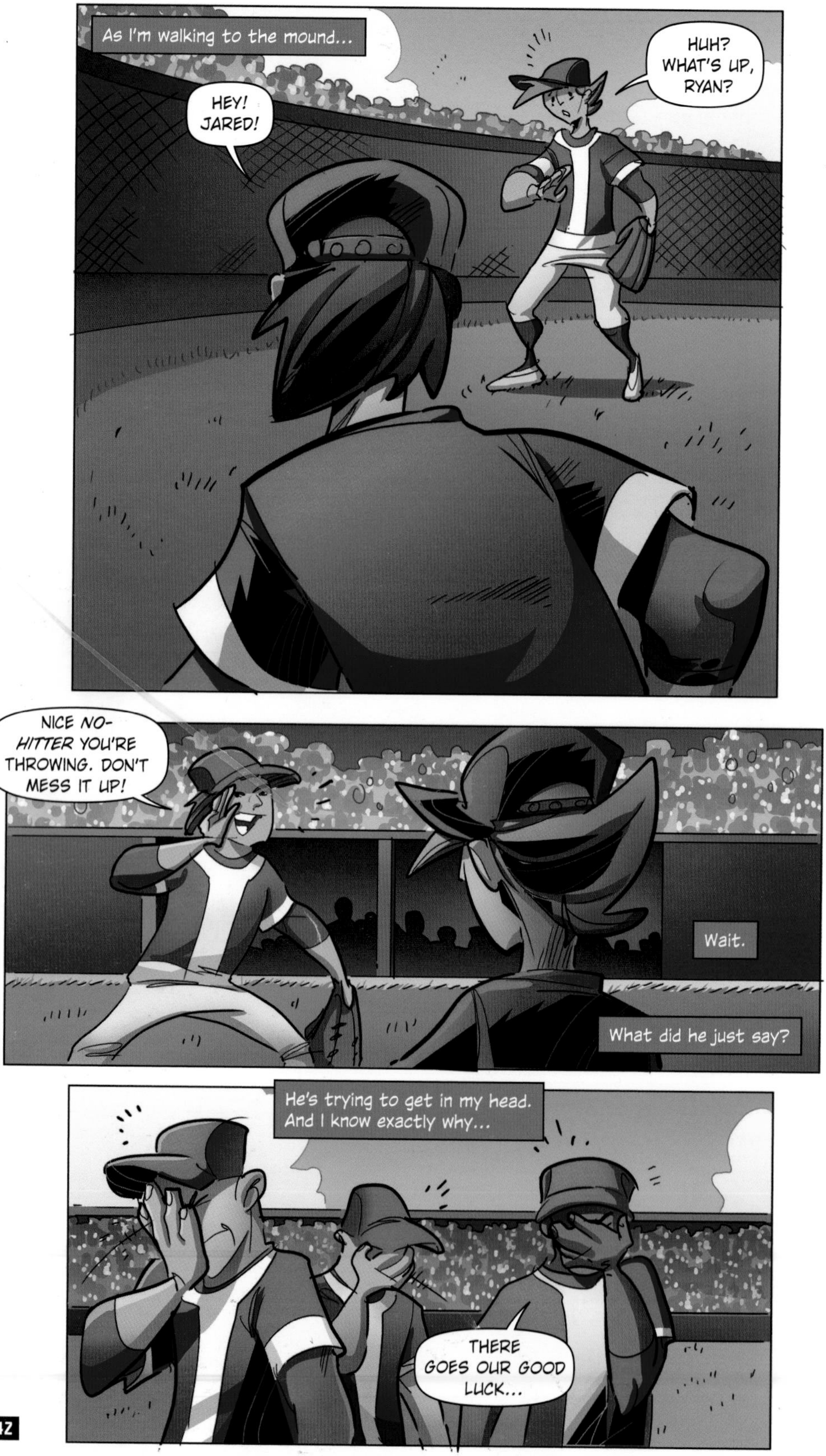
As I'm walking to the mound...
HEY! JARED!
HUH? WHAT'S UP, RYAN?
NICE *NO-HITTER* YOU'RE THROWING. DON'T MESS IT UP!
Wait.
What did he just say?
He's trying to get in my head. And I know exactly why...
THERE GOES OUR GOOD LUCK...

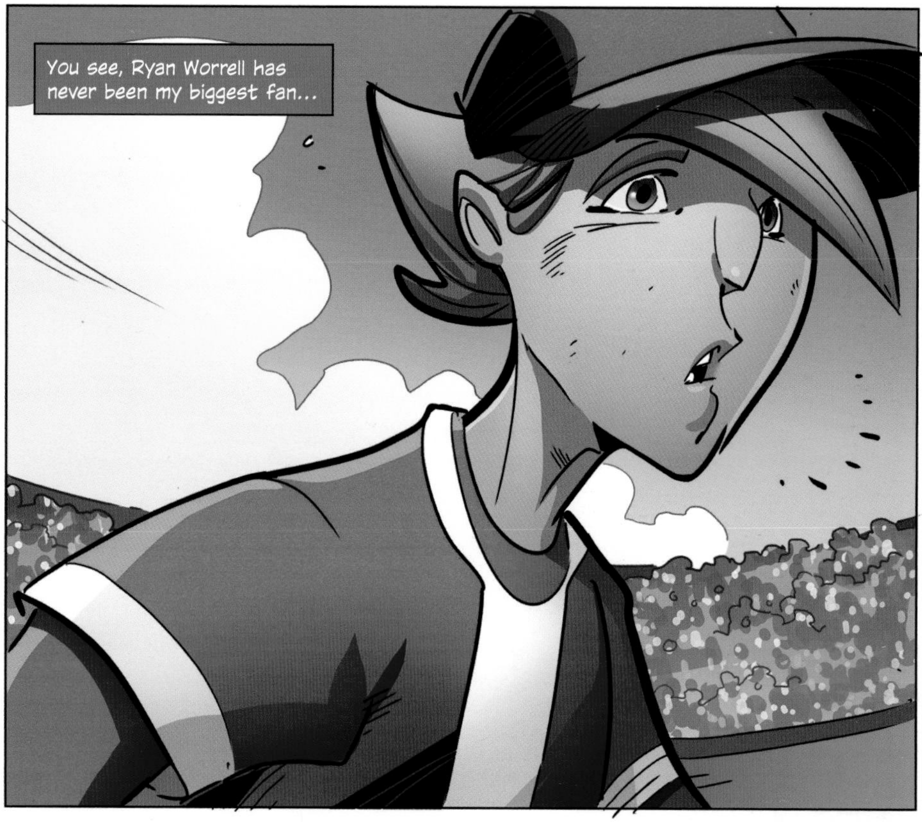
You see, Ryan Worrell has never been my biggest fan...

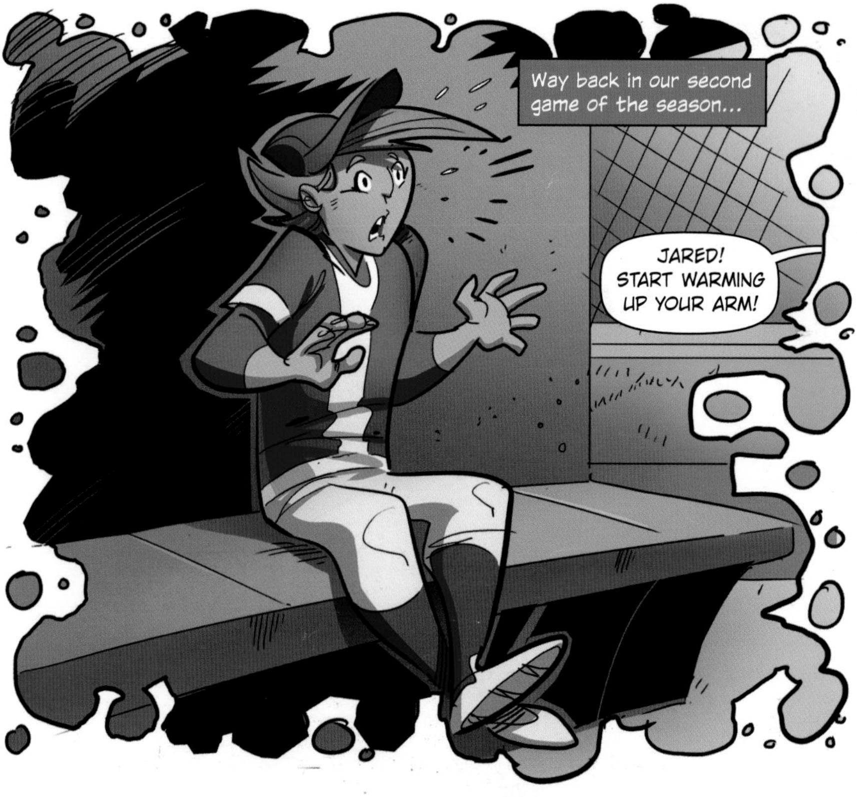
Way back in our second game of the season...
JARED! START WARMING UP YOUR ARM!

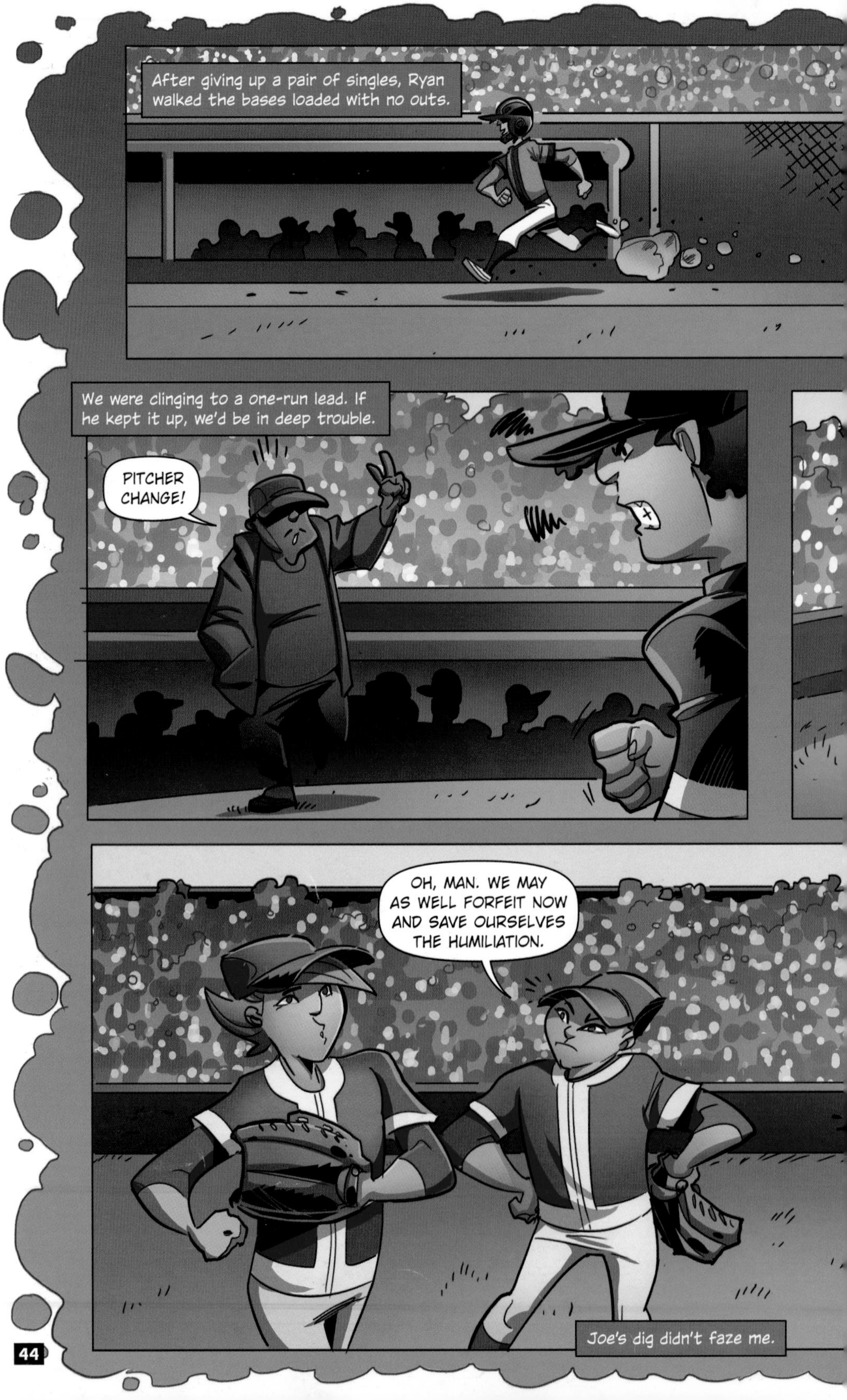
After giving up a pair of singles, Ryan walked the bases loaded with no outs.
We were clinging to a one-run lead. If he kept it up, we'd be in deep trouble.
PITCHER CHANGE!
OH, MAN. WE MAY AS WELL FORFEIT NOW AND SAVE OURSELVES THE HUMILIATION.
Joe's dig didn't faze me.

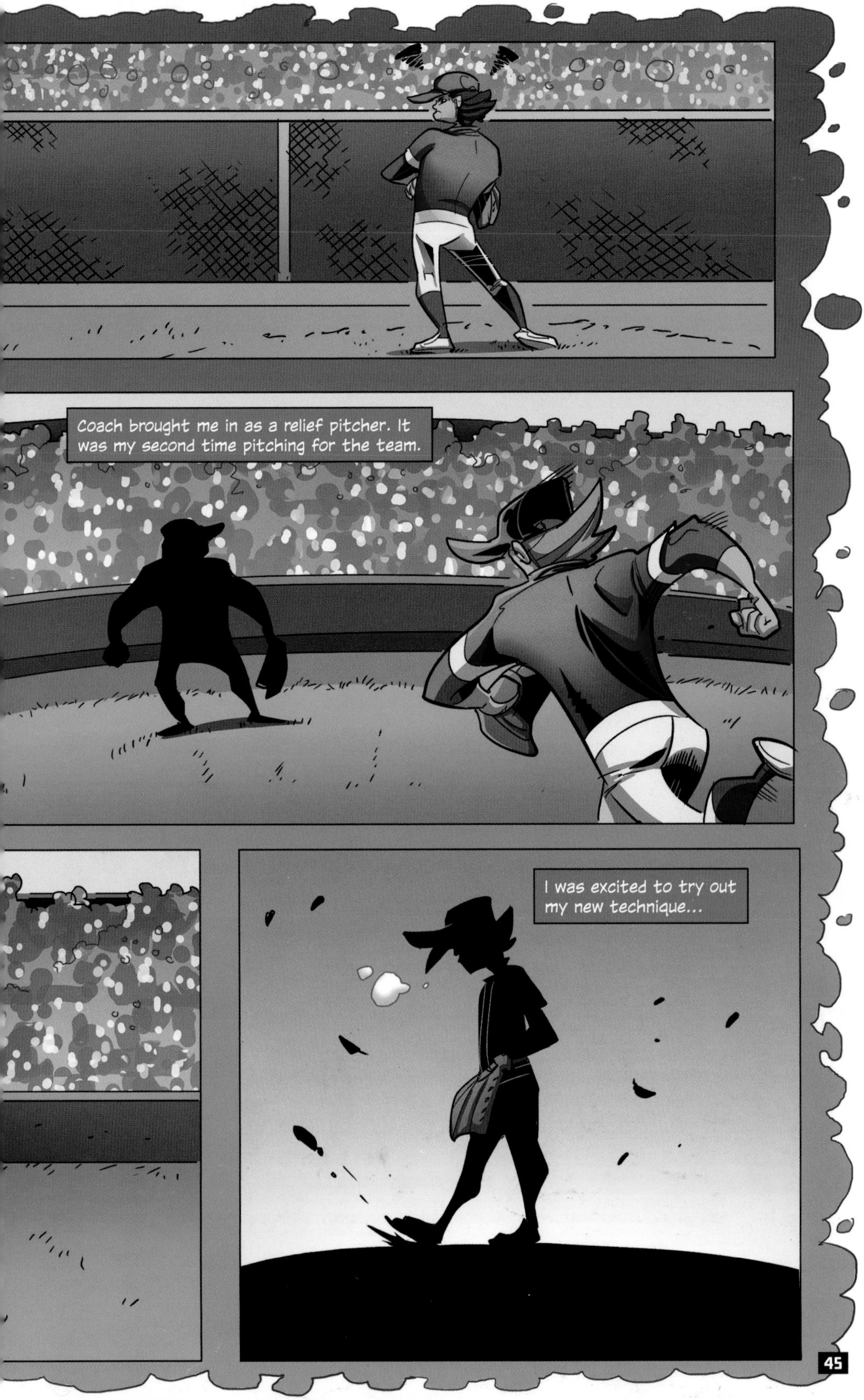

Coach brought me in as a relief pitcher. It was my second time pitching for the team.
I was excited to try out my new technique...

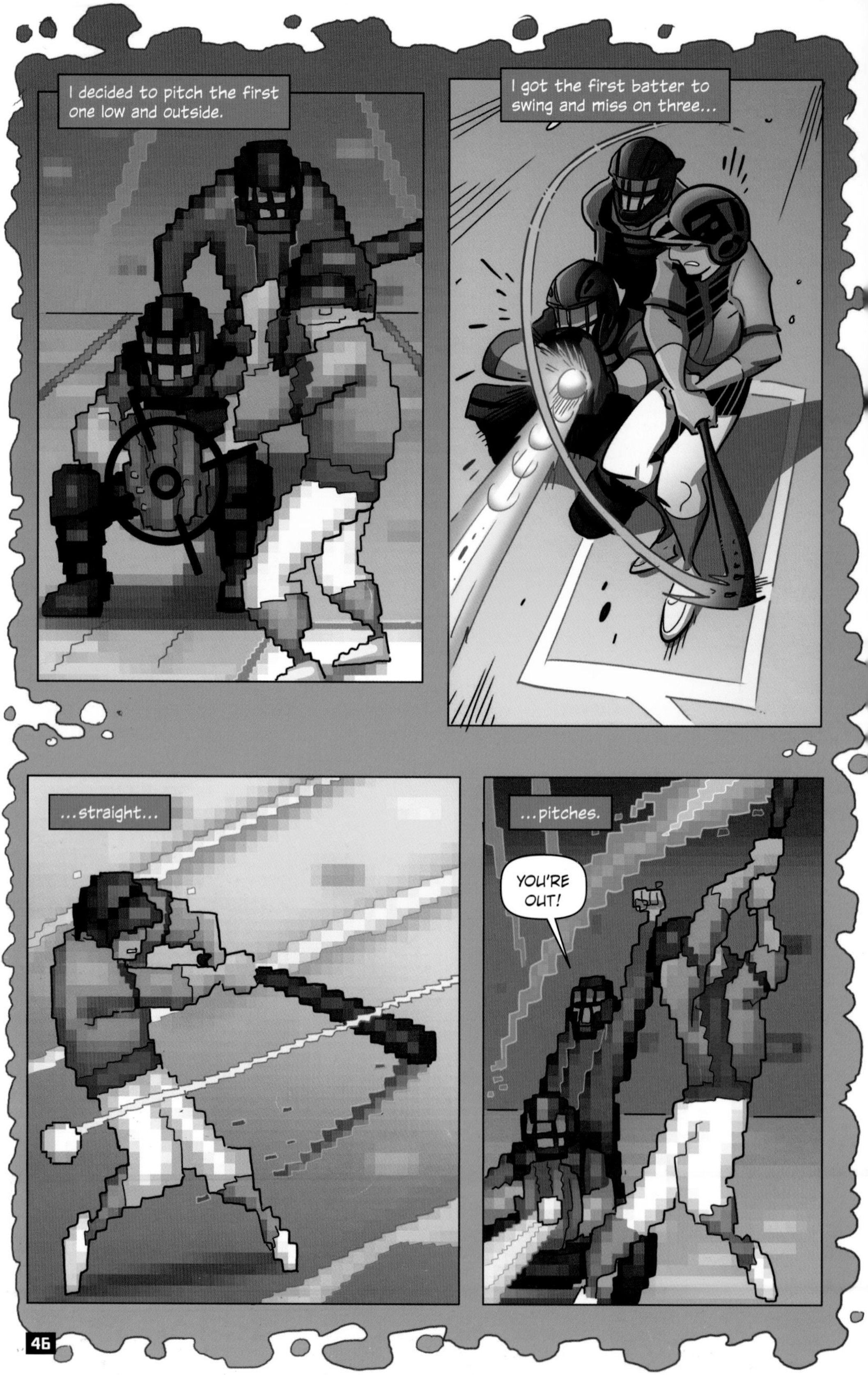
I decided to pitch the first one low and outside.
I got the first batter to swing and miss on three...
...straight...
...pitches.
YOU'RE OUT!

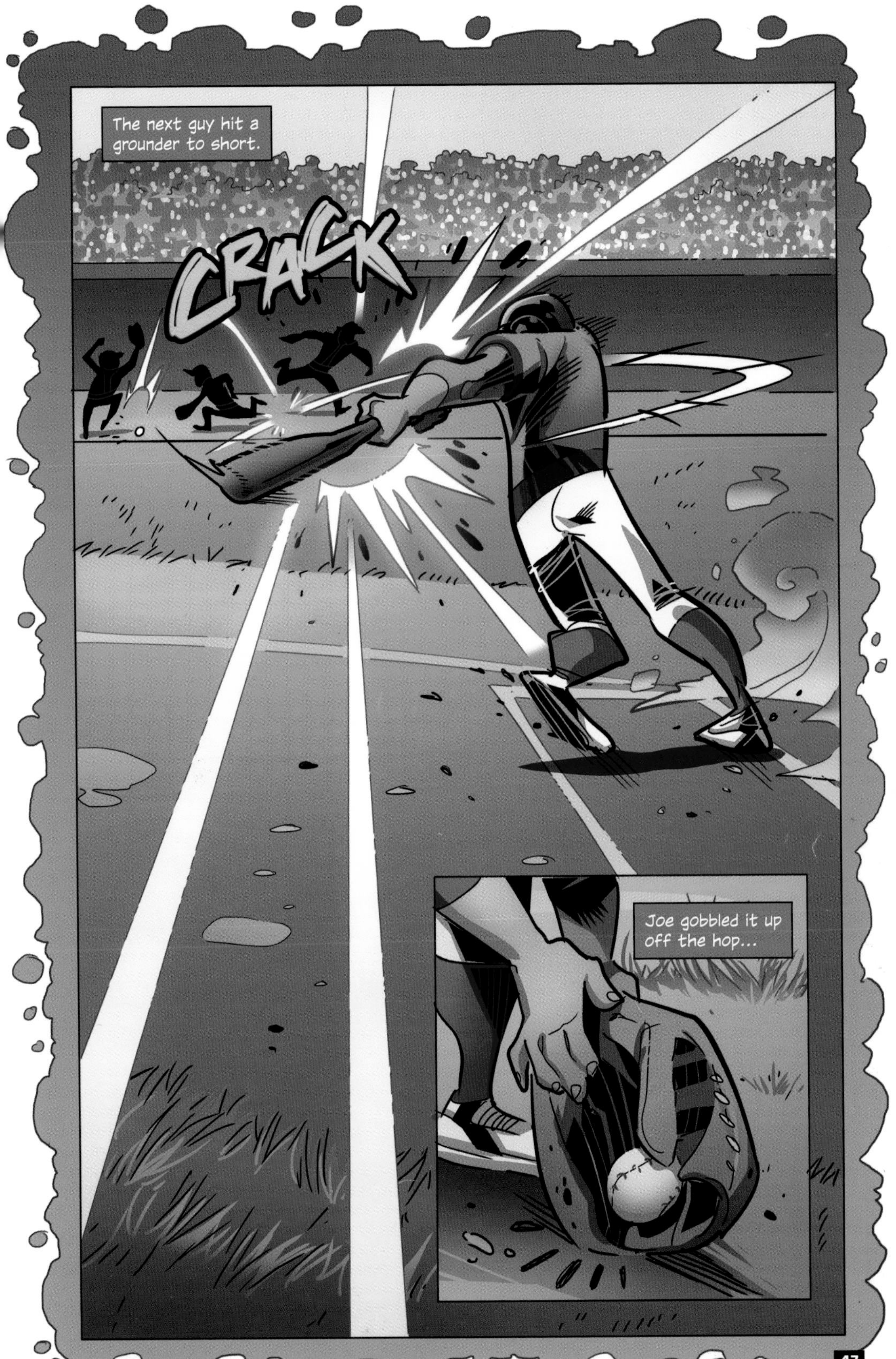
The next guy hit a grounder to short.
CRACK
Joe gobbled it up off the hop...

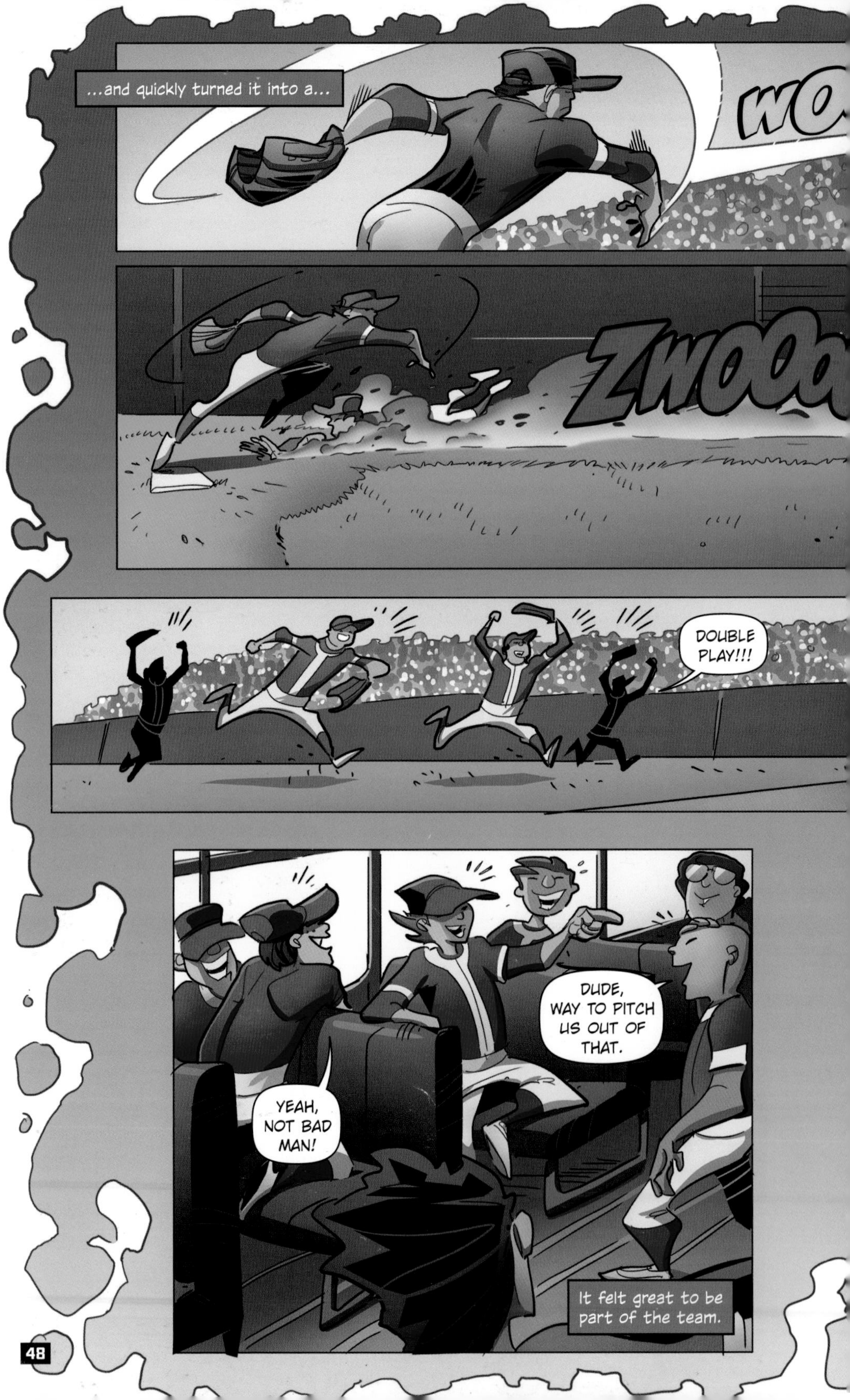
...and quickly turned it into a...
WO
ZWOOo
DOUBLE PLAY!!!
DUDE, WAY TO PITCH US OUT OF THAT.
YEAH, NOT BAD MAN!
It felt great to be part of the team.

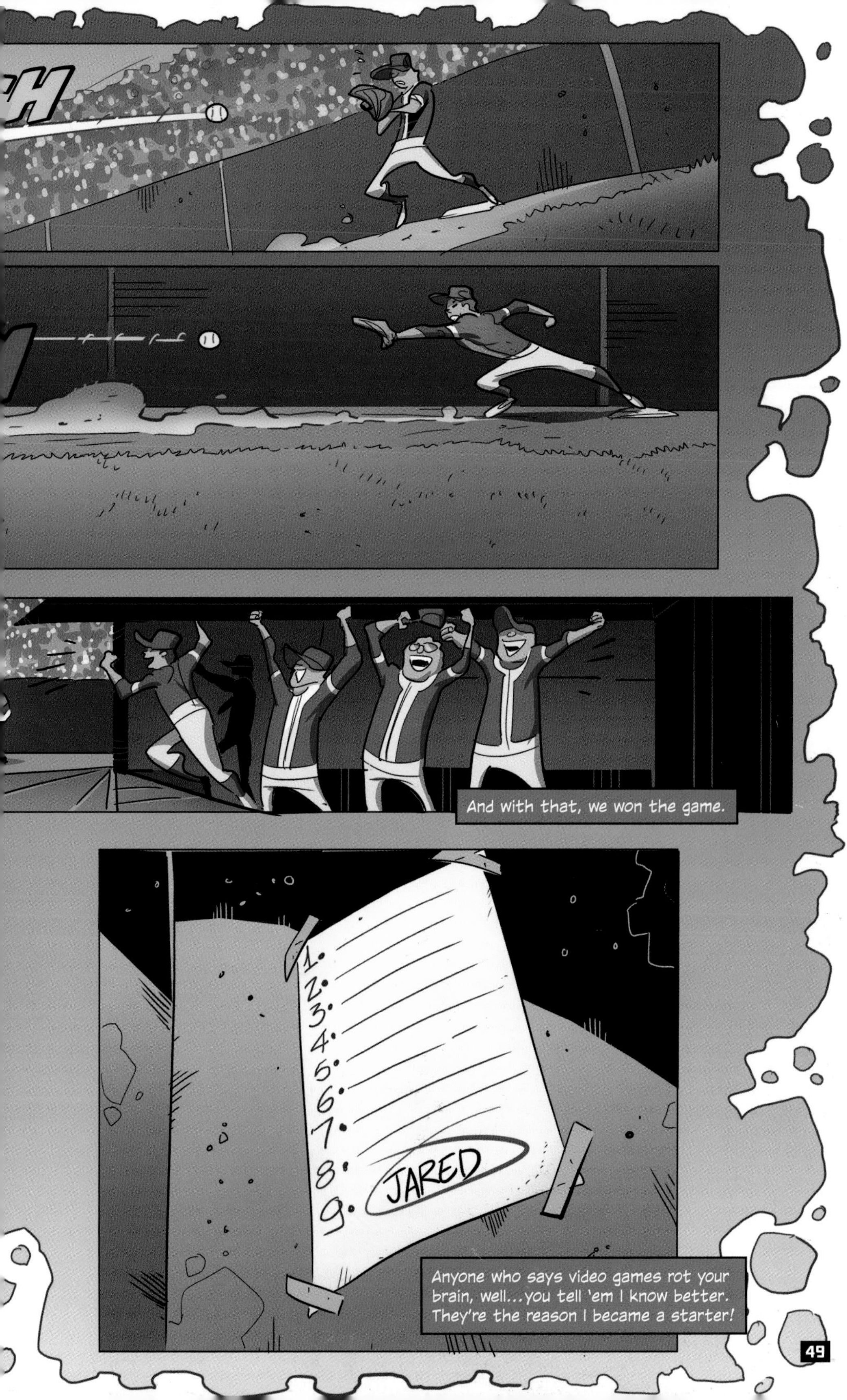
H
And with that, we won the game.
1.
2.
3.
4.
5.
6.
7.
8.
9. JARED
Anyone who says video games rot your brain, well...you tell 'em I know better. They're the reason I became a starter!

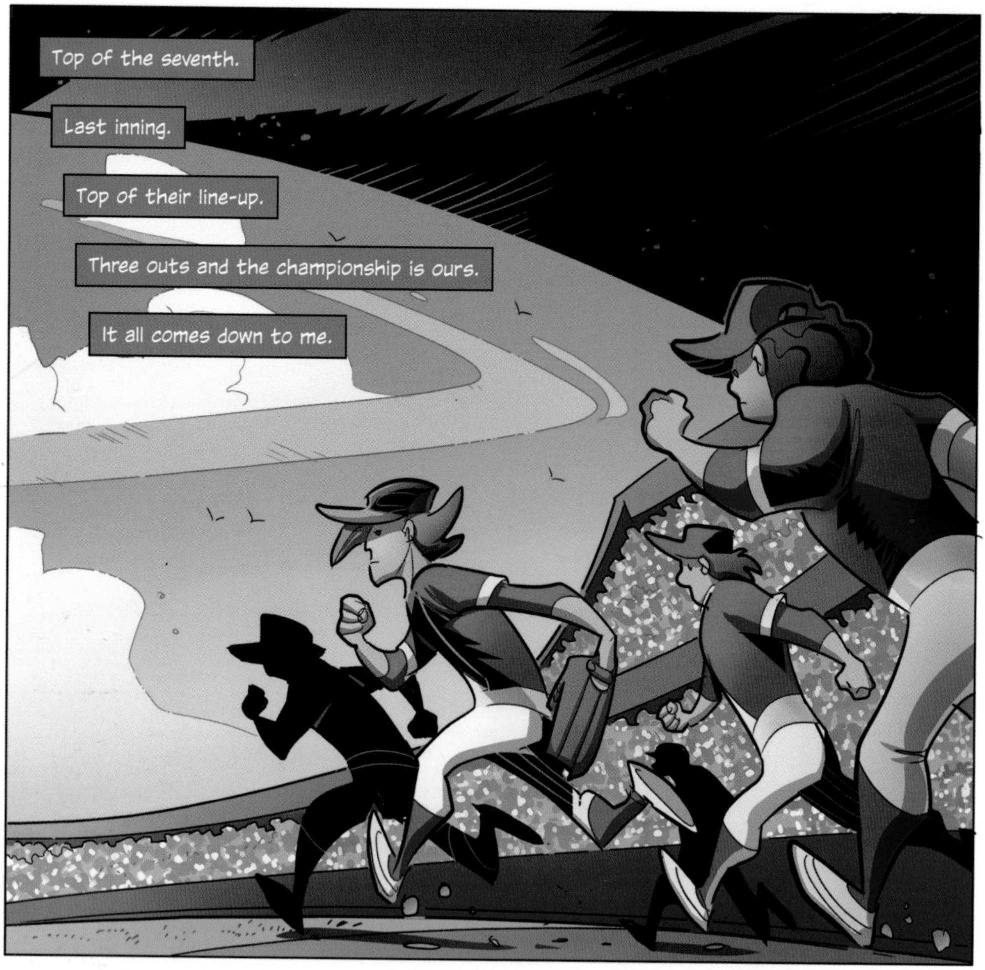
Top of the seventh.
Last inning.
Top of their line-up.
Three outs and the championship is ours.
It all comes down to me.

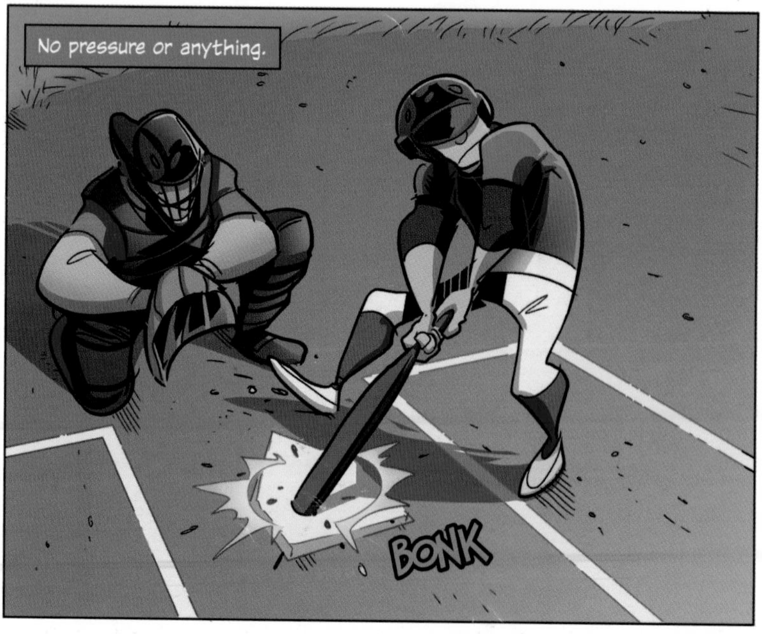
No pressure or anything.
BONK

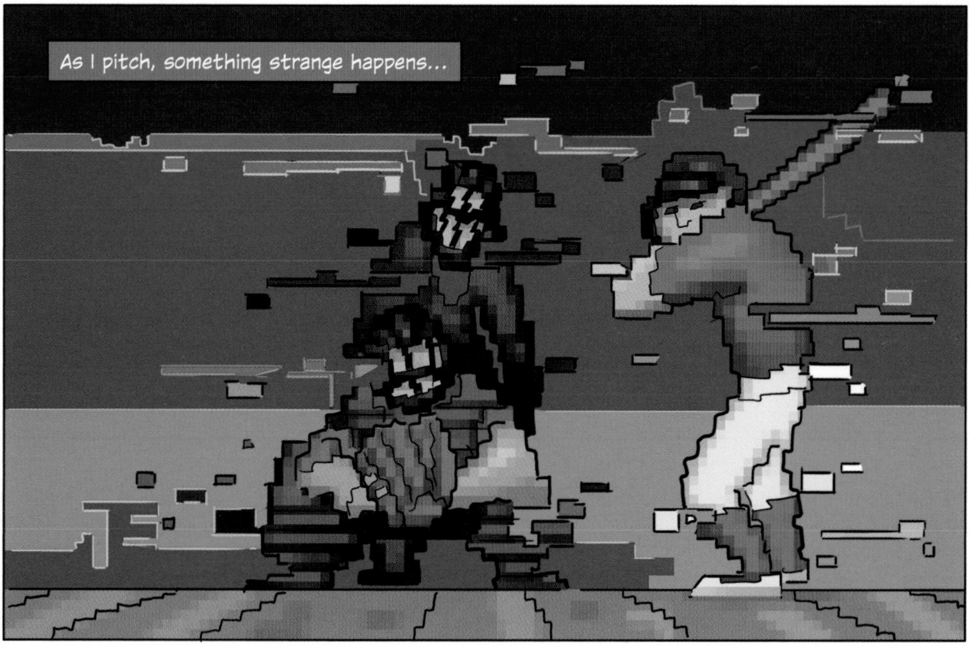
As I pitch, something strange happens...

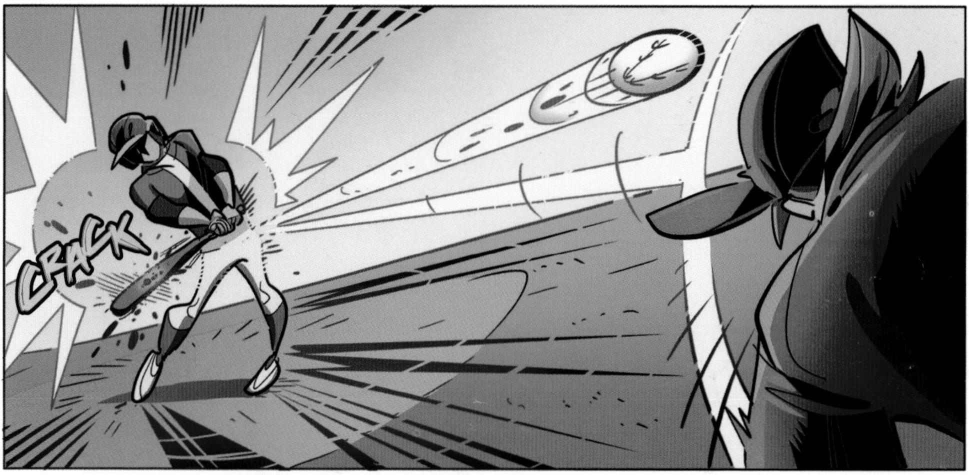
CRACK

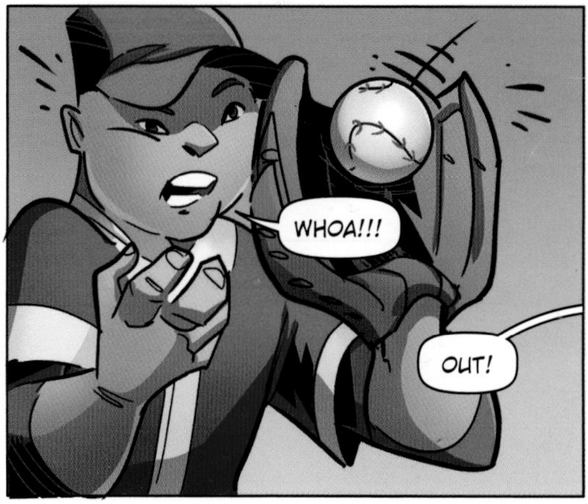
WHOA!!!
OUT!

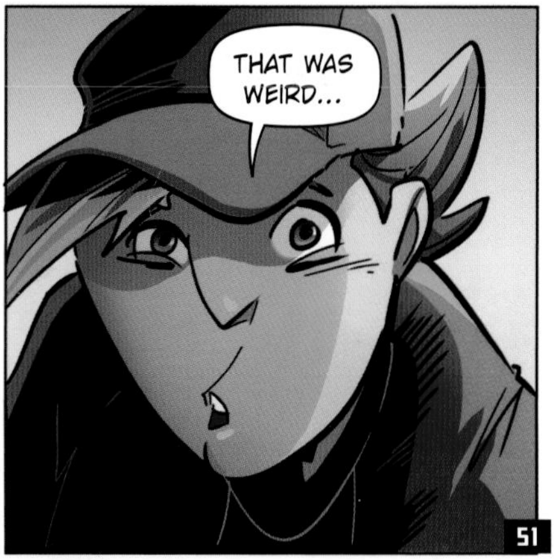
THAT WAS WEIRD...

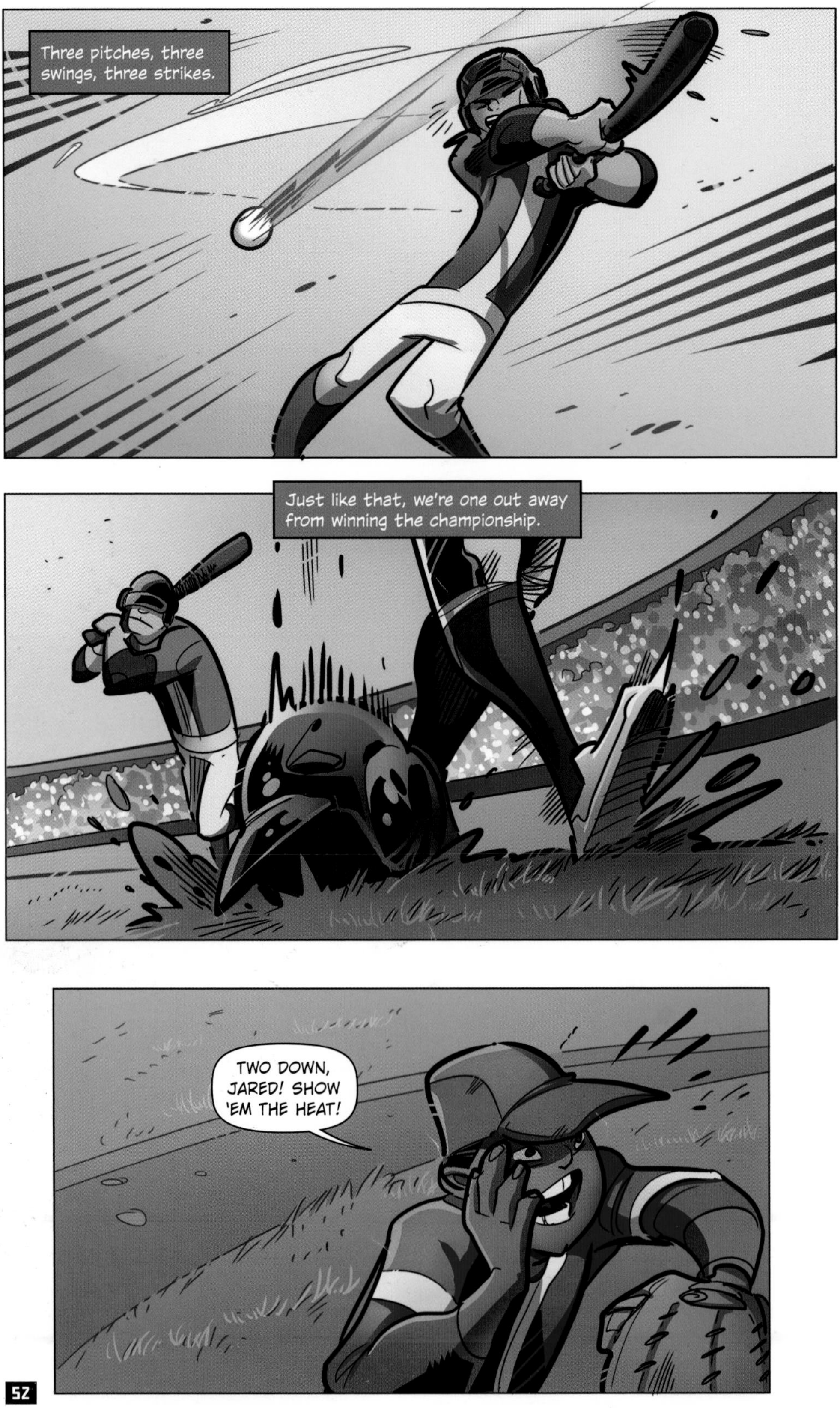
Three pitches, three swings, three strikes.
Just like that, we're one out away from winning the championship.
TWO DOWN, JARED! SHOW 'EM THE HEAT!

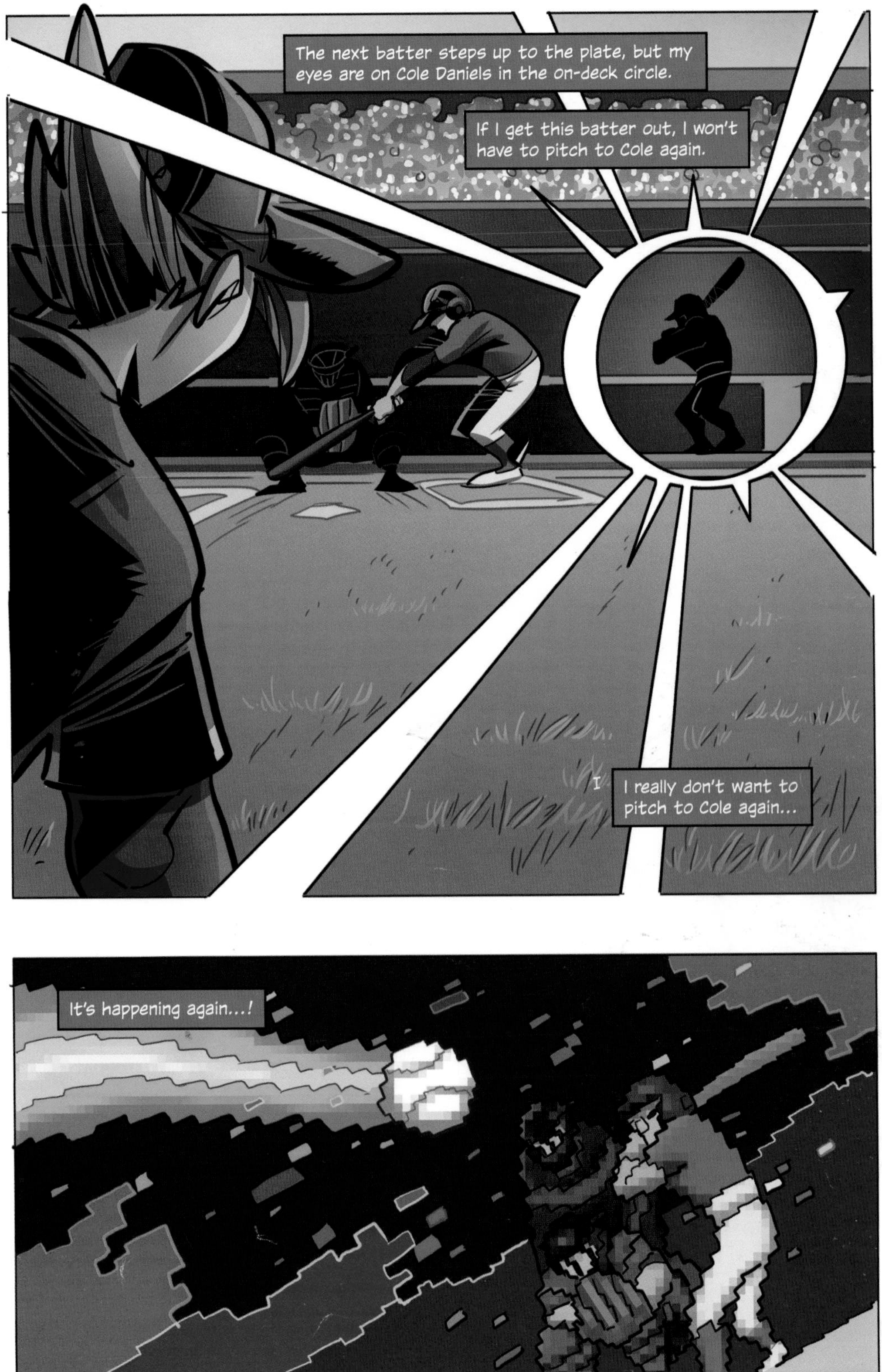
The next batter steps up to the plate, but my eyes are on Cole Daniels in the on-deck circle.
If I get this batter out, I won't have to pitch to Cole again.
I really don't want to pitch to Cole again...
It's happening again...!

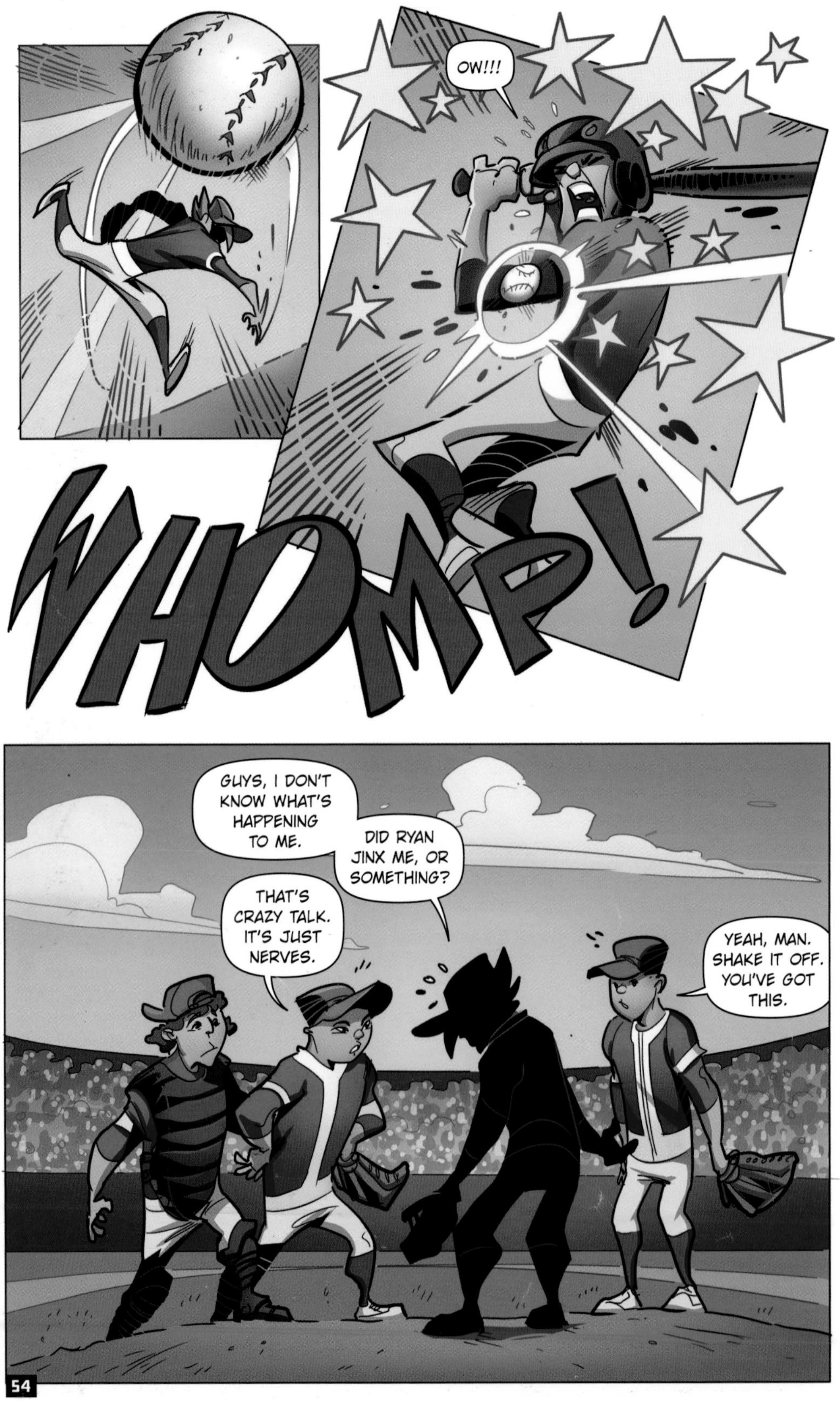
OW!!!
WHOMP!
GUYS, I DON'T KNOW WHAT'S HAPPENING TO ME.
DID RYAN JINX ME, OR SOMETHING?
THAT'S CRAZY TALK. IT'S JUST NERVES.
YEAH, MAN. SHAKE IT OFF. YOU'VE GOT THIS.

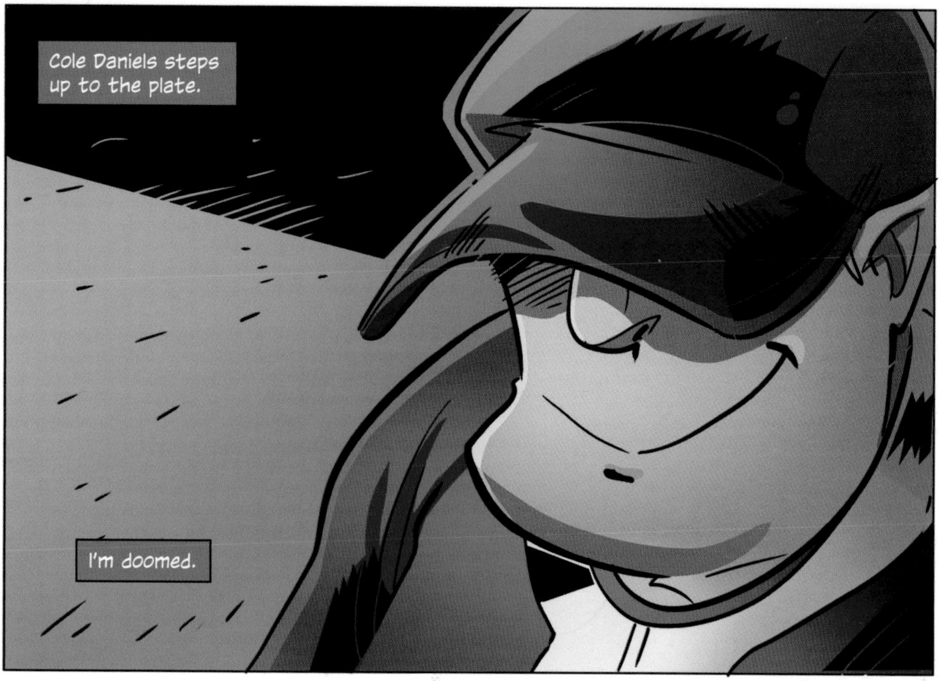
Cole Daniels steps up to the plate.
I'm doomed.

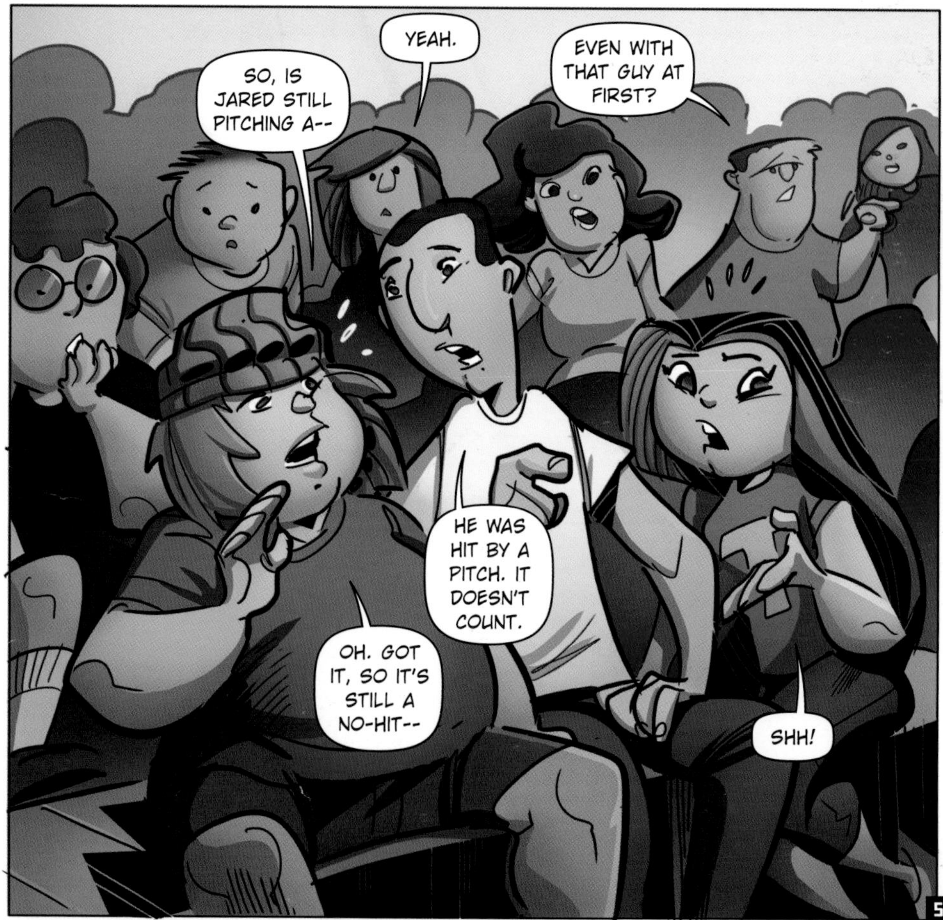
SO, IS JARED STILL PITCHING A--
YEAH.
EVEN WITH THAT GUY AT FIRST?
HE WAS HIT BY A PITCH. IT DOESN'T COUNT.
OH. GOT IT, SO IT'S STILL A NO-HIT--
SHH!

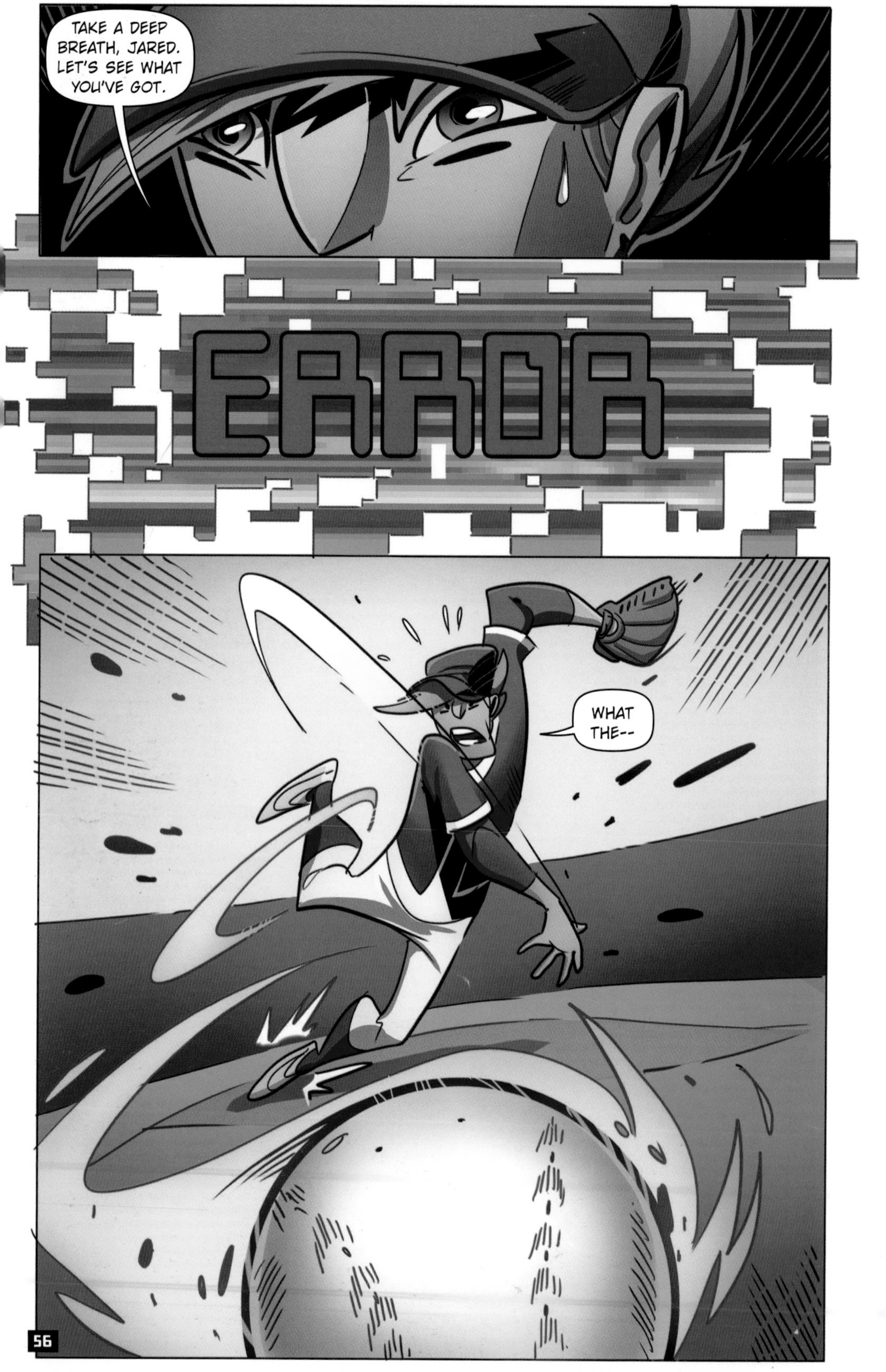
TAKE A DEEP BREATH, JARED. LET'S SEE WHAT YOU'VE GOT.
ERROR
WHAT THE--

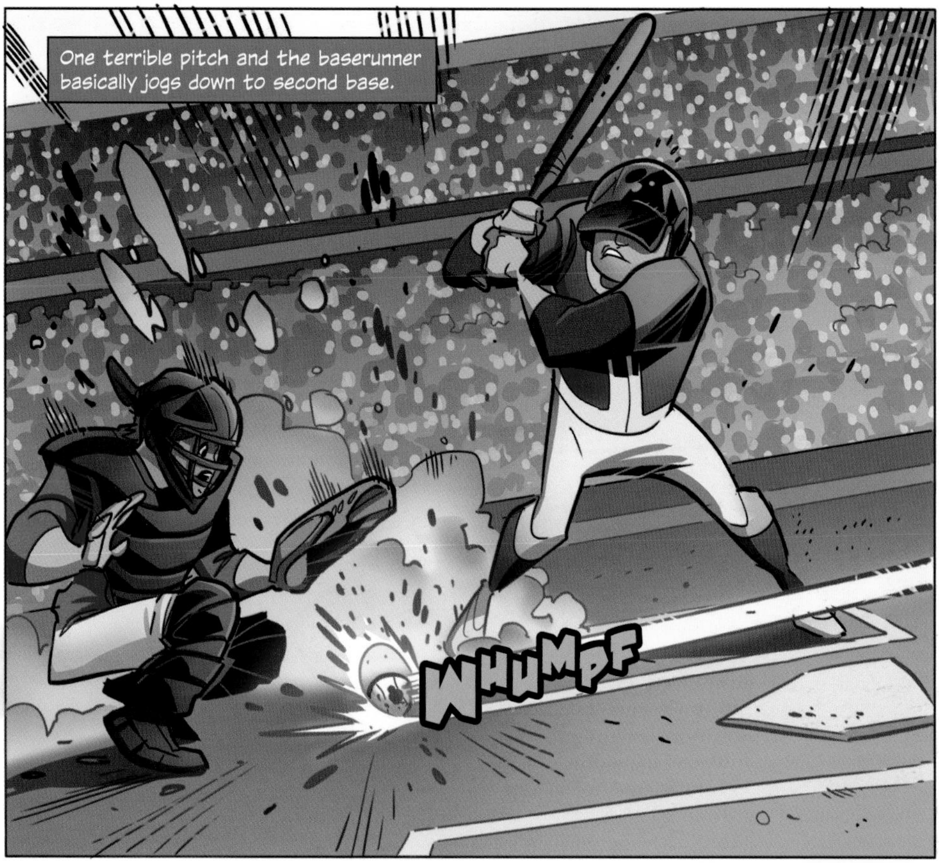
One terrible pitch and the baserunner basically jogs down to second base.
WHUMPF

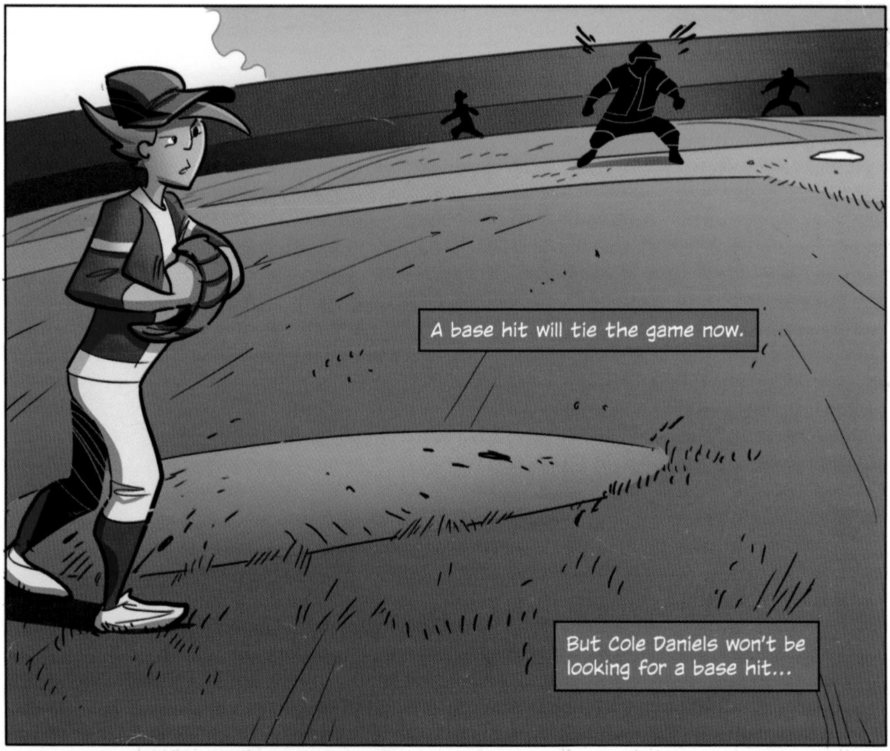
A base hit will tie the game now.
But Cole Daniels won't be looking for a base hit...

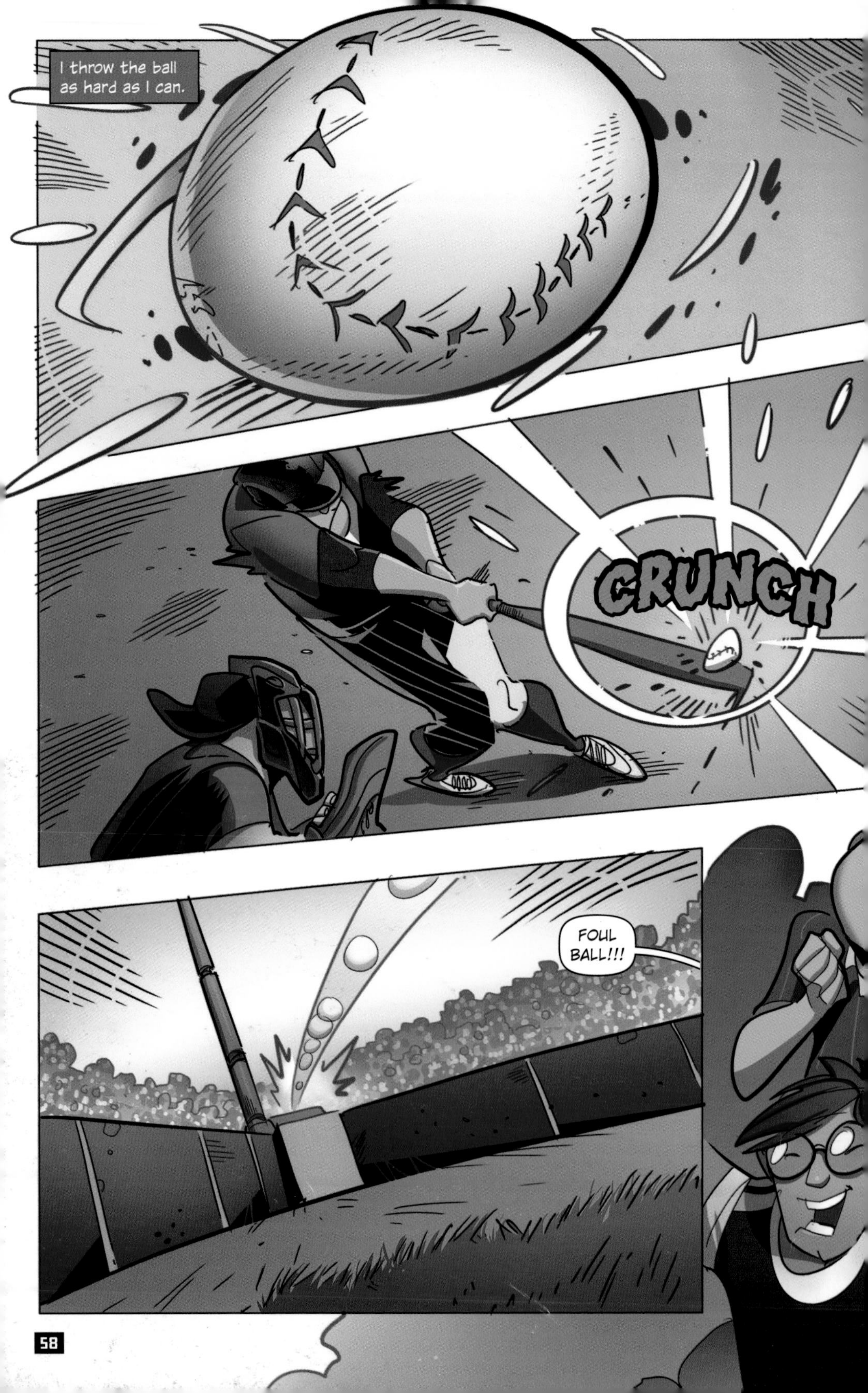
I throw the ball as hard as I can.
CRUNCH
FOUL BALL!!!

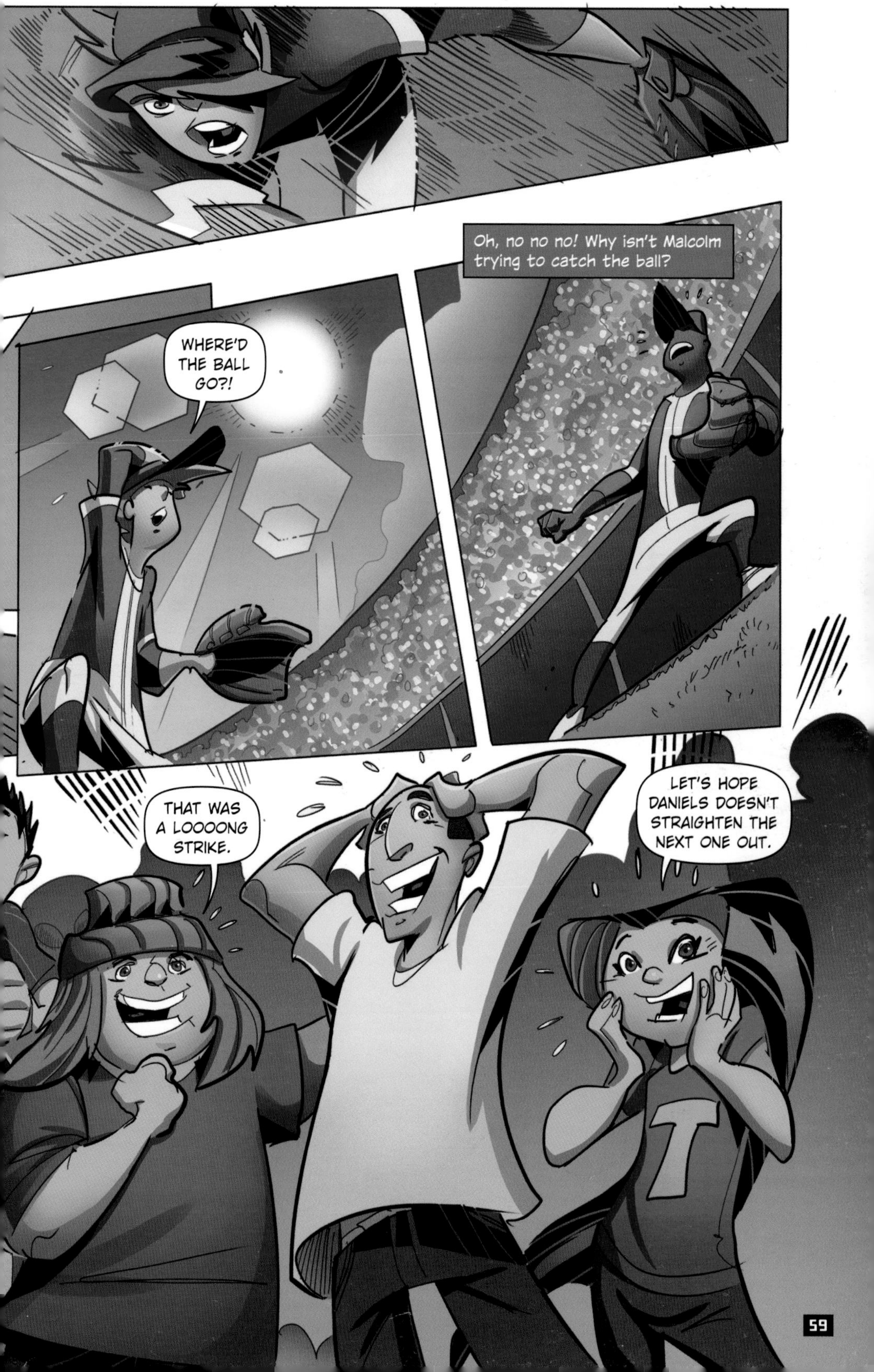
Oh, no no no! Why isn't Malcolm trying to catch the ball?
WHERE'D THE BALL GO?!
THAT WAS A LOOOONG STRIKE.
LET'S HOPE DANIELS DOESN'T STRAIGHTEN THE NEXT ONE OUT.

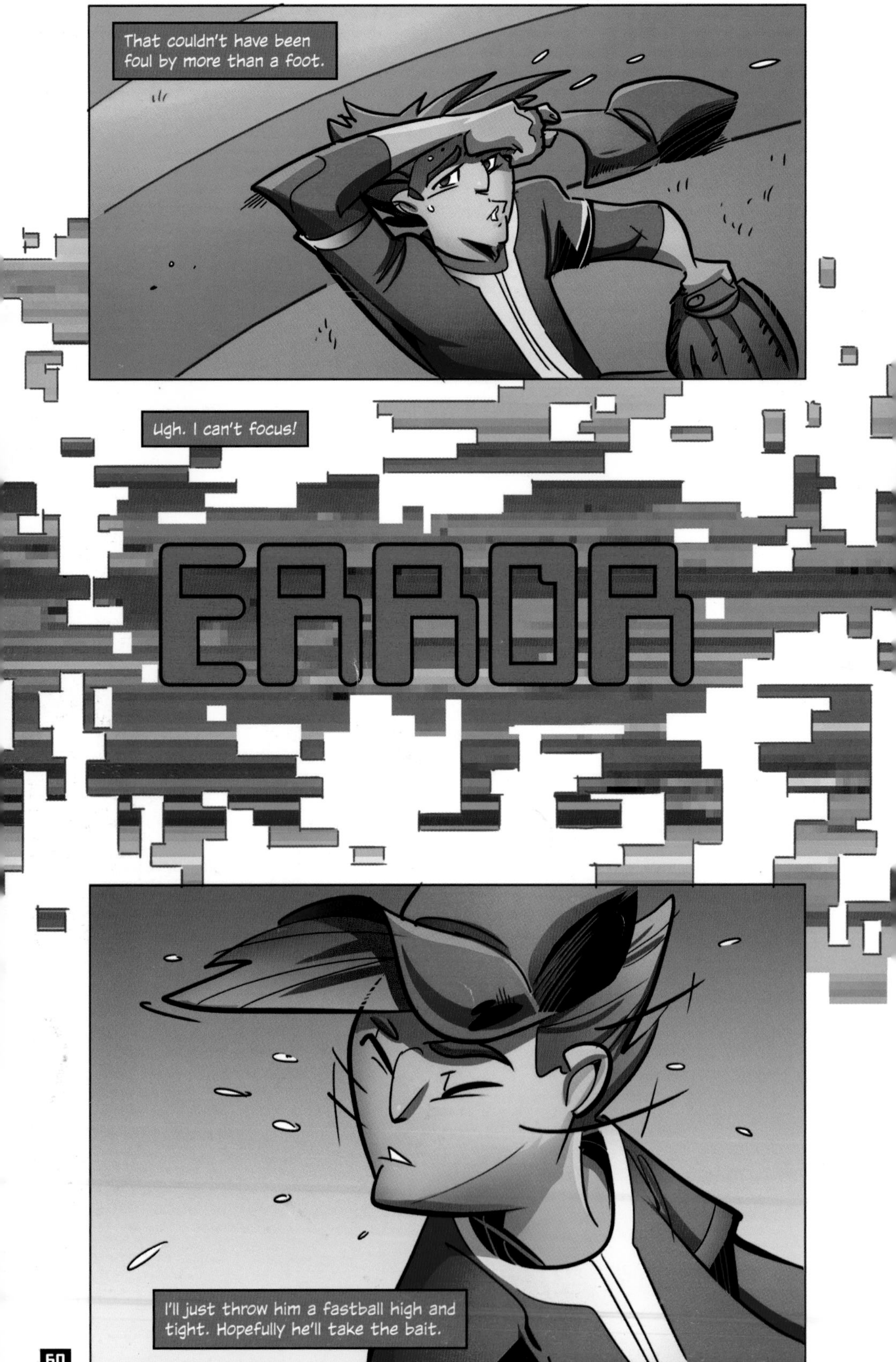
That couldn't have been foul by more than a foot.
Ugh. I can't focus!
ERROR
I'll just throw him a fastball high and tight. Hopefully he'll take the bait.

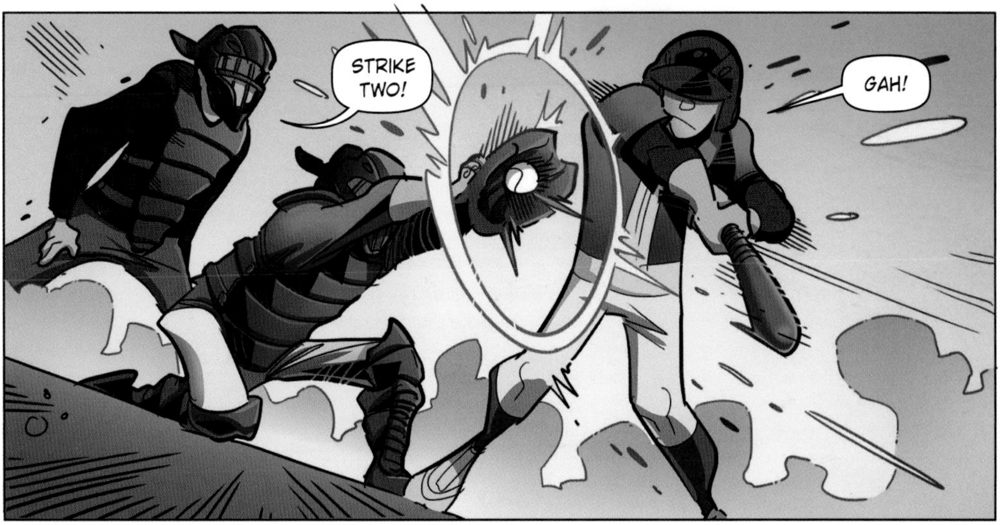
STRIKE TWO!
GAH!

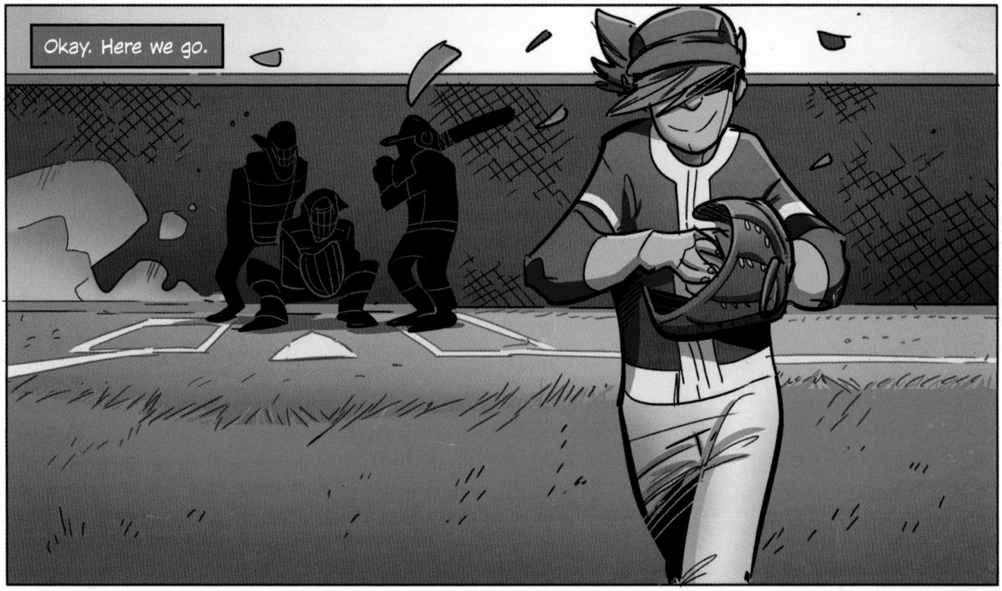
Okay. Here we go.

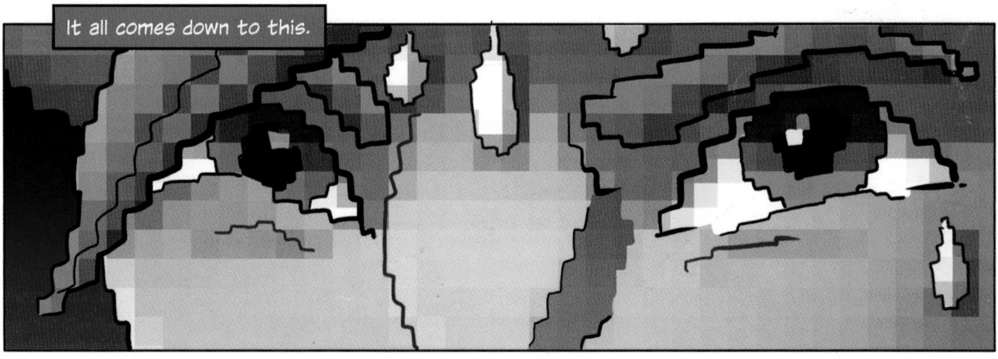
It all comes down to this.

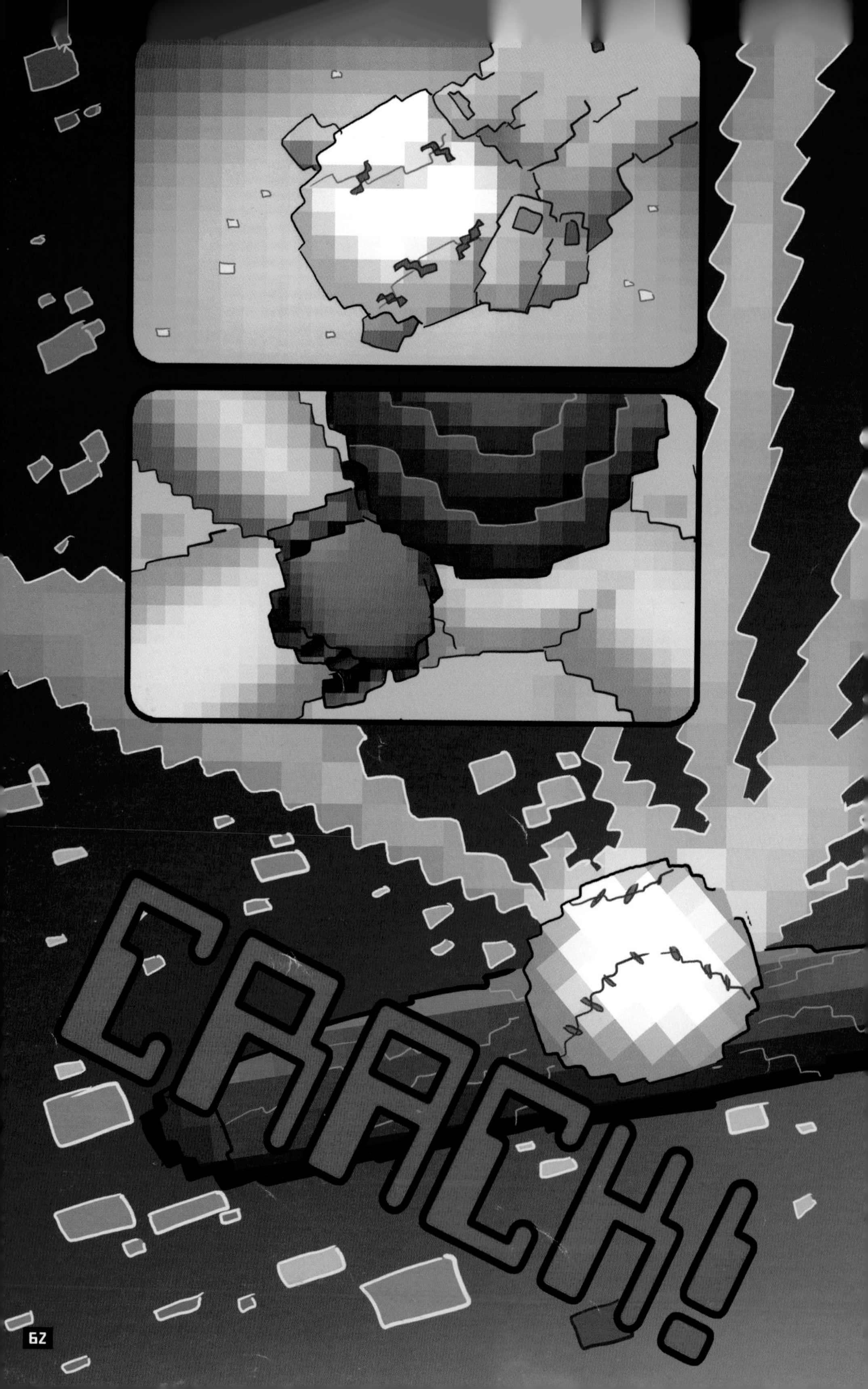
CRACK!

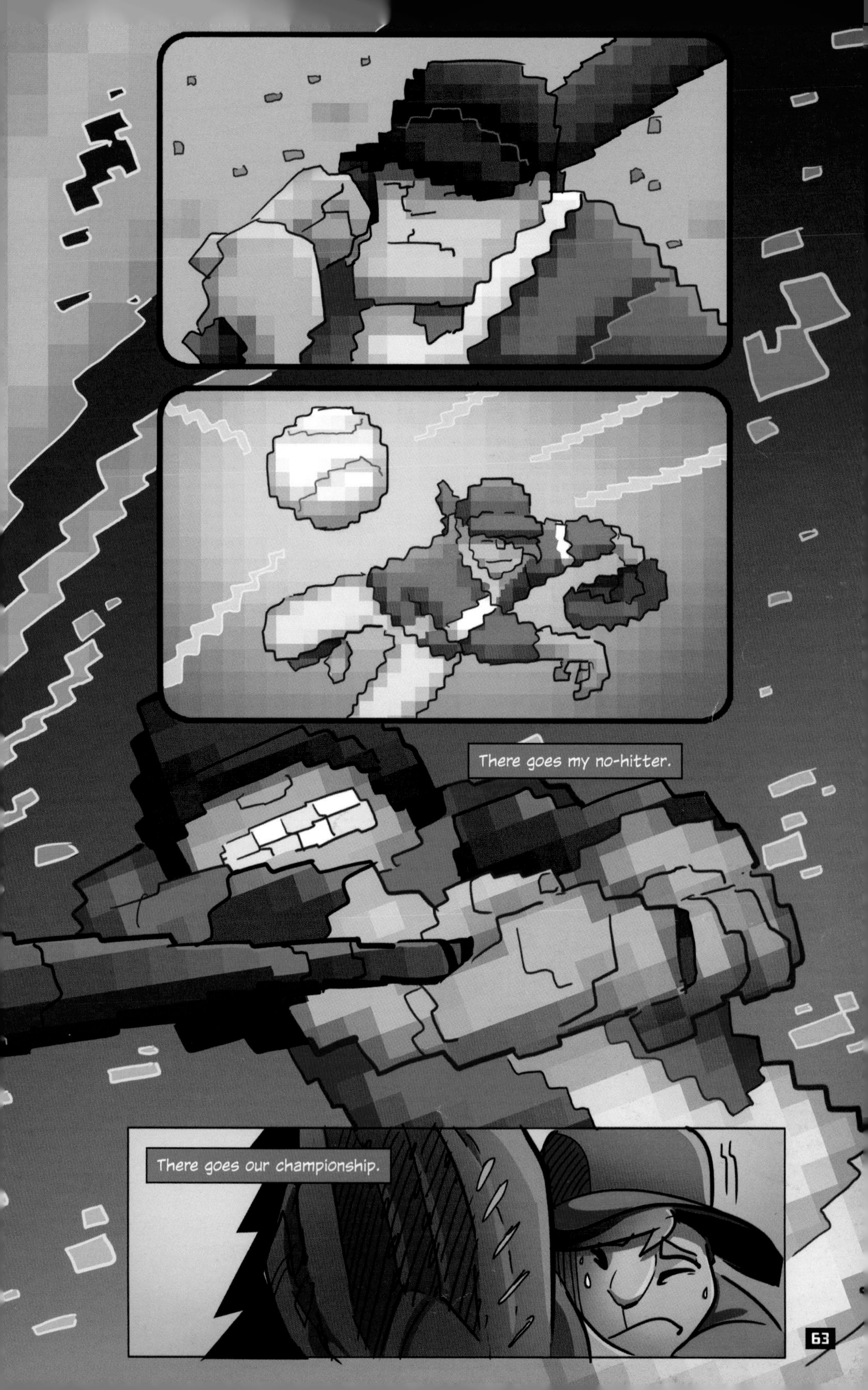
There goes my no-hitter.
There goes our championship.

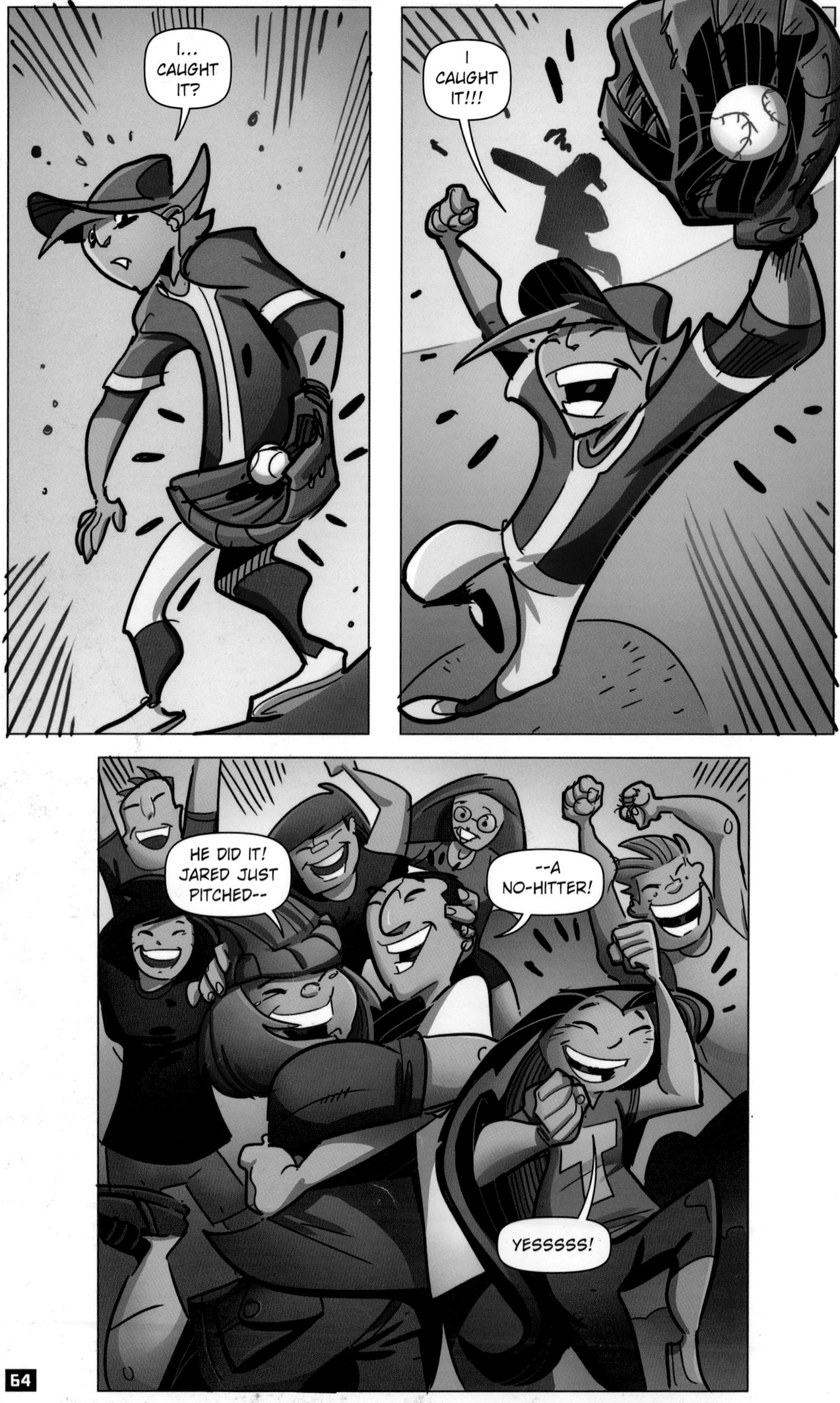
I... CAUGHT IT?
I CAUGHT IT!!!
HE DID IT! JARED JUST PITCHED--
--A NO-HITTER!
YESSSSS!

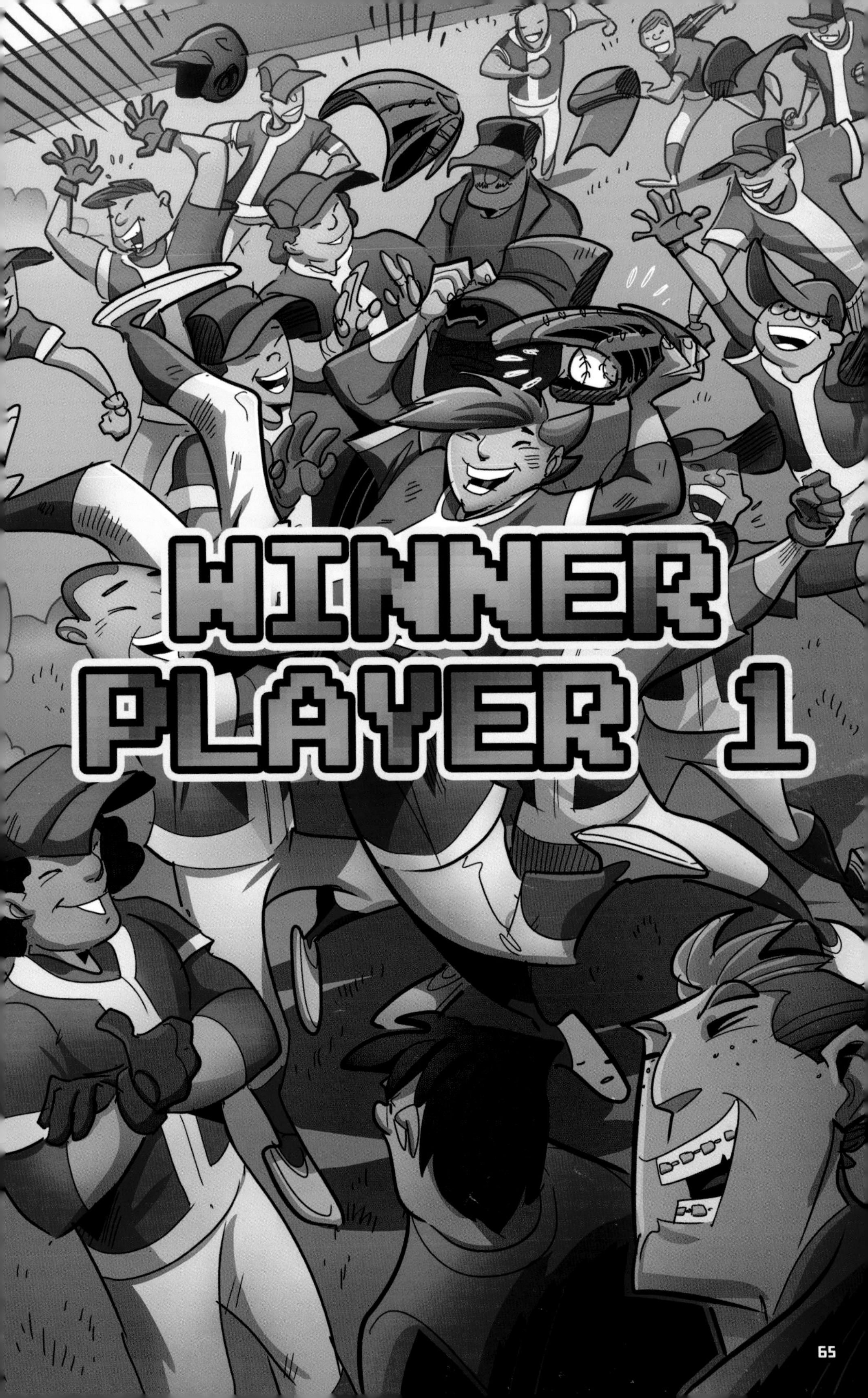
WINNER
PLAYER 1

ABOUT THE AUTHOR

BRANDON TERRELL is the author of numerous children's books, including six volumes of the Tony Hawk's 900 Revolution series and several Sports Illustrated Kids Graphic Novels. When not hunched over his laptop writing, Brandon enjoys watching movies, reading, baseball, and spending time with his wife and two children in Minnesota.

ABOUT THE ILLUSTRATOR

EDUARDO FERRARA has been drawing professionally since he was fourteen. Though best known for his work on many Star Wars books for Dark Horse, he's also illustrated a regular soccer comic strip, and he has created toy designs for Muzzi Toys and playing cards for Marvel Universe. He lives in Sao Paolo, Brazil.

ABOUT THE LETTERER

JAYMES REED has operated the company Digital-CAPS: Comic Book Lettering since 2003. He has done lettering for many publishers, most notably and recently Avatar Press. He's also the only letterer working with Inception Strategies, an Aboriginal-Australian publisher that develops social comics with public service messages for the Australian government. Jaymes also a 2012 & 2013 Shel Dorf Award Nominee.

GLOSSARY

ACCURACY (AK-yur-uhss-ee)—if you have good pitching accuracy, you are able to consistently throw the ball where you want

BUNT (BUHNT)—a bunt occurs when a batter loosely holds the bat in front of the plate and gently taps the ball into play

CURVEBALL (CURV-ball)—a pitch thrown with spin to make it curve downward and to the side

DISTRACTED (diss-TRAK-tid)—unable to think, pay attention, or concentrate on something

EXHAUSTED (ig-ZAWSS-tid)—completely fatigued or worn out

FATE (FATE)—something unavoidable

FAZE (FAYZ)—if something fazes you, it makes you feel afraid or uncertain

FORFEIT (FOR-fit)—to lose or give up (something), often due to breaking a law or rule

HUMILIATION (hyoo-mil-ee-A-shuhn)—the state of feeling ashamed, embarrassed, or foolish

INSTINCTS (IN-stinkts)—things you know without having to learn or think about

JINX (JINKS)—if you jinx someone, you give them bad luck

OFFICIAL (oh-FISH-uhl)—if something is official, it is established to be true

SAC BUNT (SAK BUHNT)—a sac bunt, or sacrifice bunt, occurs when a batter lays down a bunt to move a baserunner ahead at the cost of an out

SUPERSTITION (soo-per-STISH-uhn)—the belief that certain actions are good or bad luck

VISUAL QUESTIONS

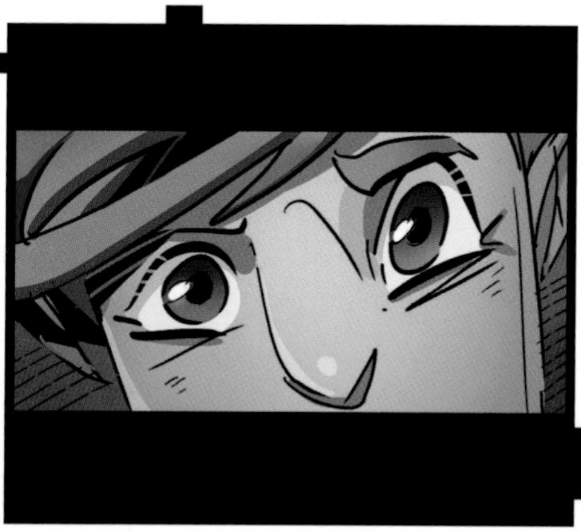

1. In this panel, the comic's creators decided to do a close-up of Jared's face. How does this panel make you feel? Why do you think the creators chose to illustrate the panel in this fashion?

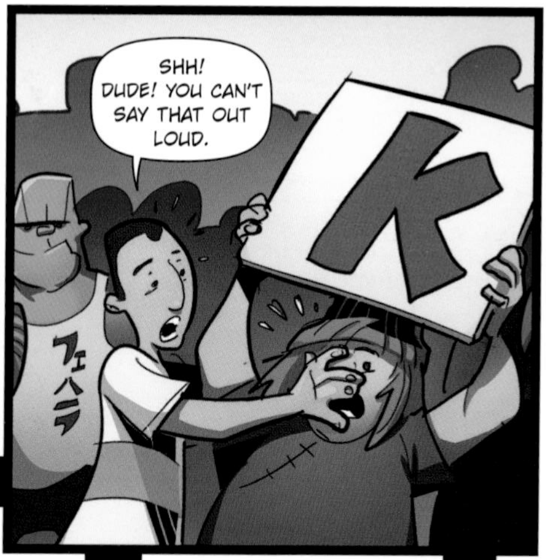
SHH!
DUDE! YOU CAN'T SAY THAT OUT LOUD.
K

2. In this book, several characters express that they are superstitious, or believe that certain actions can create good or bad luck. Do you believe in good or bad luck? Do you consider yourself to be superstitious? Why or why not?

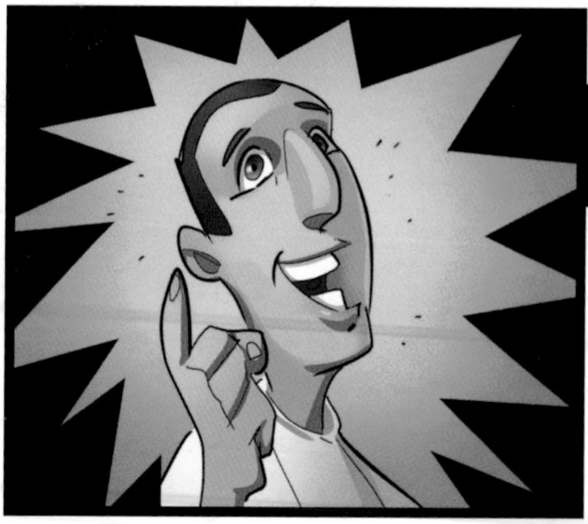

3. In this panel, we see a starburst-like shape behind Oscar's head. Why did the comic book's creators decide to do this?

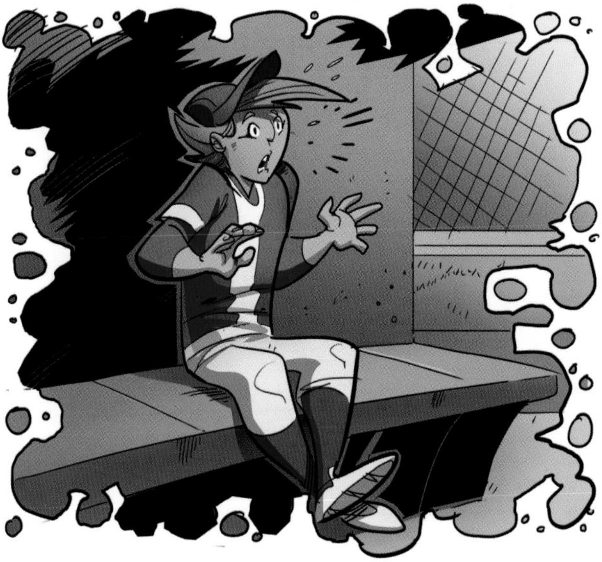

4. Why does this panel have cloud-like borders? If you aren't sure, reread page 43 for clues.

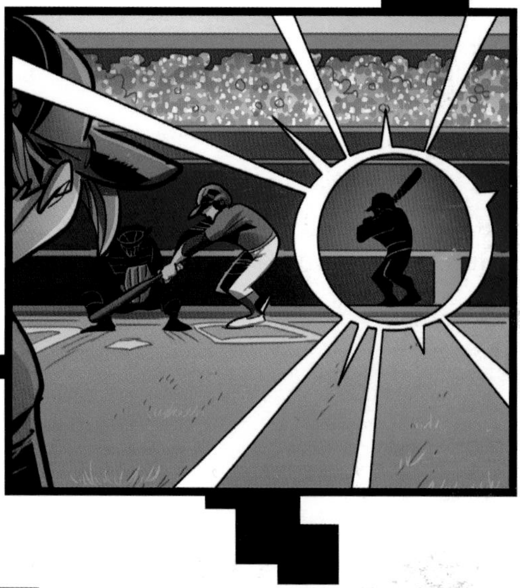

5. We see a circle focused around Cole Daniels, who is in the on-deck circle. Why do you think the illustrator chose to draw the panel in this manner?

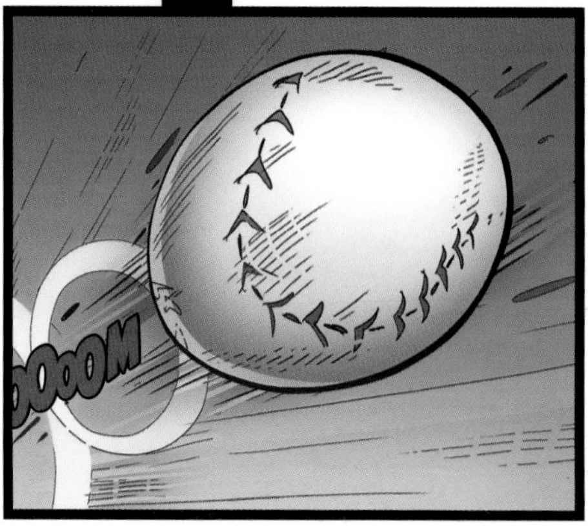
OOOOM

6. The baseball in this panel is warped horizontally a little. Why did the illustrator do this? How does it improve the action in the comic?

AD THEM A

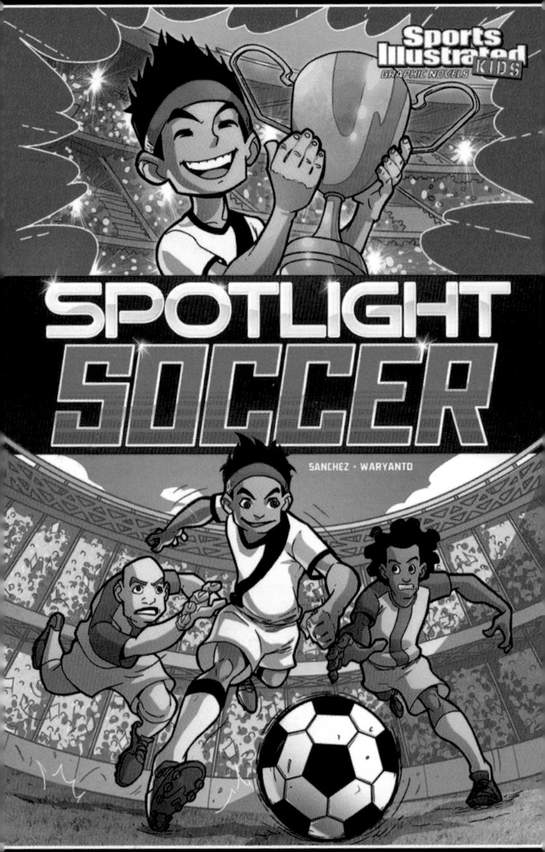
Sports Illustrated KIDS
GRAPHIC NOVELS
SPOTLIGHT
SOCCER
SANCHEZ · WARYANTO

CCER

ning else, Franco dreams of going pro some day. A the best kind of player—more giving than greedy, ts instead of scoring goals. And that method work ange schools. On his new team, Franco's pass-firs working. To make matters worse, the team is filled doesn't seem to care about anything. Franco refus pro die, but the new team is pretty much a living n

Sports Illustrated KIDS
GRAPHIC NOVELS
QUARTERBACK RUSH
BOWEN · GARCIA

QUARTERBACK RUSH

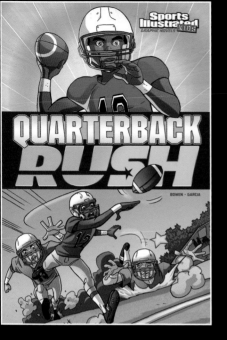

The Otters are absolutely awesome in practice. Everyone's talented and determined, and their new quarterback, Aaron Corbin, throws bullets . . . so why are the Otters struggling to win games? Steve Michaels, one of the team's receivers, notices that Aaron seems to be afraid of getting hit. With a little help from his teammates, Steve goes to great lengths to toughen up Aaron only to discover that toughness isn't the quarterback's actual problem.

Sports Illustrated KIDS
GRAPHIC NOVELS
BEASTLY BASKETBALL
JOHNSON · GARCIA

BEASTLY BASKETBALL

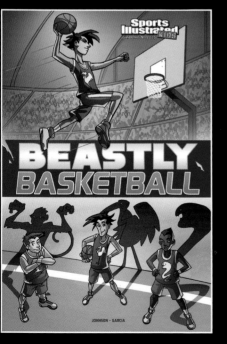

Joe knows kung fu. In fact, he loves it more than anything. Every single evening, Joe walks to his neighborhood kung fu studio to practice for hours on end . . . until the day he arrives to find his studio has closed—permanently. So, Joe decides to pursue his second-favorite activity—basketball. He joins his school's team only to find that the players are disorganized, timid, and lacking in discipline! So, Joe uses his experience in martial arts to bring out the best—or beast!—in his teammates! Will their newfound skills lead to flawless victory, or will they continue to get beaten to the punch?

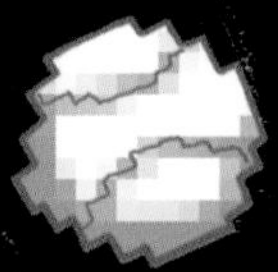

GAME OVER